Always Alex

By
Robin Alexander

ALWAYS ALEX
© 2014 BY ROBIN ALEXANDER

All rights reserved. No part of this book may be reproduced in printed or electronic form without permission. Please do not participate in or encourage piracy of copyrighted materials in violation of the author's rights. Purchase only authorized editions.

ISBN 13: 978-1-935216-61-2

First Printing: 2014

This Trade Paperback Is Published By
Intaglio Publications
Walker, LA USA

WWW.INTAGLIOPUB.COM

This is a work of fiction. Names, characters, places, and incidents are the product of the author's imagination or are used fictitiously, and any resemblance to actual persons, living or dead, businesses, companies, events, or locales is entirely coincidental.

CREDITS

EXECUTIVE EDITOR: TARA YOUNG
COVER DESIGN BY: Tiger Graphics

Dedication

For Maw Maw.

Acknowledgments

As always, I am grateful to Tara and my editorial team, who routinely make voodoo dolls in my honor.

And to Becky, my love, who forgives me when I fail to complete a sentence because my mind has wandered into its imaginary world.

Prologue

Alex listened as her coin made a splash in the water. She closed her eyes and exhaled loudly as she made her wish. "Okay, it's done."

"What'd you wish for?"

"For the well to stop stinking." Alex pinched her nose.

"No, really." Dana grabbed the front of her shirt and gazed up at her with bright blue eyes. "Did you wish for love?"

Alex shook her head and looked away. "We're not supposed to tell, or it won't come true."

Dana released her and danced in a circle, arms flailing, dishwater blond hair bouncing around her face. "I gotta tell you mine. I wished to marry Kevin Hartford."

Alex wondered if the quarter she threw in the well would make her wish stronger since Dana only tossed in a dime. "Yuk. He looks like a bulldog."

Dana stopped twirling, and her face darkened. "Take it back."

"No, it's true."

"Take it back, Alex," Dana yelled, her face red with anger.

"Lower your voice before Old Man Wicker finds us out here." Alex put her hands on her hips. "You're sixteen not six. That 'take it back' shit is stupid. I'm just telling you how I feel. Kevin looks like a dog and acts like a dog, so he must be a dog. If you screw him, you might have puppies."

Dana jutted her chin defiantly. "I have."

Alex did her best not to show it, but inside, her heart was breaking. "You're lying."

"You've done it. Don't look at me like I'm a baby, you're only two years older."

Alex swallowed hard. "Tell me you're lying."

"I can't. I almost hope I get pregnant. Kevin promised to marry me if I did," Dana said as she looked away.

Alex forced herself to ask the question she wasn't sure she wanted to know the answer to. The words felt bitter on her tongue. "Do you love him?"

Dana kicked dirt at the well. "No, but I'll do anything to get away from my dad. You're going off to school in a few months. What do I have left?"

"Come with me," Alex said, her voice raspy with emotion.

"You know he'll come get me if I did." Dana turned and looked at Alex. "Why do you look so sad?"

Alex uttered a partial truth. "I don't want to leave." She couldn't admit to her best friend that she'd just crushed her heart by giving herself to someone else for all the wrong reasons.

Chapter 1

"Watch your speed."

Sydney Elliot stared at the road as the latest of her mother's warnings went ignored.

"I said watch your speed. I can't afford for you to get another speeding ticket. If you're not going to listen to me, pull over and I'll drive."

Sydney scowled as her foot lightened up on the accelerator.

"You can give me the silent treatment all you want, but it isn't going to change a thing. I'm not any happier about this move than you are." Dana stared out the window as she watched fields and trees fly by. "The last thing I ever wanted to do was return to Barbier Point. We're broke. Trust me when I say that if there were any other options, we would not be moving in with my father."

"I don't even know him. I'd rather live in a cardboard box on the street."

Dana felt the same way. If she had been alone, she might've considered living out of her car. As a single mother, however, she had Sydney to think about. Desperate measures were required. Every ounce of pride that Dana still had was pushed way down deep when she'd called her father and asked to come back home. She loved him, but she did not like him, and she was certain that he felt the same way about her. When her mother, the mediator, had died, Dana and Daniel Castilaw drifted further apart. At first, there was the occasional phone call, then that eventually stopped. He never approved of anything she did, and there was little they could discuss without it turning into an argument. Dana didn't know how she was going to survive living with him until she could get back on her feet financially and could afford to move back to New Orleans.

"I know you had no choice," Sydney said with resignation. "But couldn't we have found a cheaper apartment?"

"We were in the cheapest I could find. Even working two jobs, there was still more money going out than was coming in. I've maxed out all my credit cards, and that was the safety net."

"I could quit school and—"

"Absolutely not. You've got one year of high school left. I just need time to get some of my debt paid down."

"File bankruptcy, we'll go on food stamps."

"No." Dana rubbed her forehead wearily. It wasn't her pride that wouldn't allow her to ask for that kind of help. In her mind, those programs were for people who had no other means, no options. She at least had one left, and she'd taken it. She leaned back in her seat and stroked Sydney's short brown locks. "Just inhale and scream at the top of your lungs. It might make you feel better."

Sydney shook her head.

"Okay, I will." Dana inhaled deeply and released a rolling scream that made Sydney jump. It seemed to go on forever as she tried to purge the desolation she felt inside.

Sydney glanced at Dana when she quieted. "Better?"

"No." Dana screamed again, and this time, she stomped the floorboard. Her voice was hoarse when she said, "Now that...I think that one helped. You try."

Sydney grinned and shook her head.

"Why?"

"Because I might cry, and I don't want to."

Dana put her hand on Sydney's shoulder. "Me either, but it's right in the center of my chest, know what I mean?"

Sydney swallowed hard and nodded. "What's in Barbier Point?"

"Not much. It's on Vermillion Bay. There are a lot of boats, old houses...trees. I don't suspect it's changed very much. When I was a kid, there was this old place that had a wishing well. Actually, it was just a hole with a bunch of bricks stacked around it, the water inside stunk, and it was full of mosquitoes. My best friend and I would sneak out there and make wishes when the old man that owned it wasn't around."

Sydney grabbed her ball cap from the console and put it on her head backward to keep her mother out of her hair. "What did you wish for?"

Dana's hand dropped back into her lap. "Puppies, a candy fountain, silly stuff when I was little. I always told my wishes, that's probably why they didn't come true. Alex would never tell me hers. She was two years older than me, and I thought I was going to die when she went away to college. After that, my wishes were to get out of Barbier Point."

"What's Grandpa like?"

Dana smiled wryly. "Consider everything I am, then think the opposite. Dad and I are like oil and water, we don't mix at all. The house is big, though, two stories. I imagine we'll have the whole top floor to ourselves. You'll have your own room, but we'll have to share a bathroom."

"Oh, joy."

"That's right, piggy. You're gonna have to learn to put your things up because I can't deal with clutter. But the rooms are huge, plenty of space for you to spread out." Dana sat up straighter. "The turn is coming up soon."

"Has Grandpa ever met me?" Sydney asked as she slowed.

"We used to visit a lot when you were a baby, but the last time he saw you was at your grandmother's funeral. You were three then."

Sydney glanced at her. "Did you and him have a big fight then or something?"

Dana stared at the road. "Your father and I had just broken up, I'd lost Mom. I'd hoped...well, I thought things might be different between us, but they weren't. With Mom gone, it just got worse." Dana pointed. "Okay, you see that white car up ahead? That's where you're going to turn."

Sydney slowed and made a right. "Oh, boy, more woods. Wait, there's a cow...that's new."

"Your sarcasm has been noted."

"Sorry." Sydney blew out a sigh. "I wanna get a job this summer."

Dana gazed at Sydney's profile. In looks, she was her father's child with her slightly upturned nose, huge brown eyes, and a few freckles on olive skin. Troy Elliot wasn't much taller than Dana's five foot six inches, but Sydney was almost six feet with a lanky build. Dana knew the height had come from her father. As far as personality went, Sydney was all Dana, but in her late teens, she'd grown out of the tomboy stage. So far, Sydney had not. She preferred her hair short, her bangs long and swept toward her face. A ball cap was usually on her head, and most of the sleeves had been cut out of her T-shirts. Sydney either wore jeans or cutoffs and detested sandals and flip-flops. Only Converse sneakers were allowed on her feet.

"I'm not opposed to you working, but when you go back to school, that will be the priority. We're about to roll into Barbier Point. You need to slow to a crawl or you'll miss it."

Time had forgotten Dana's hometown like she had. The old drugstore was still the first building as they drove down Cypermort Street, the main drag through town. The diner had been remodeled and enlarged, and the gravel parking lot was full of pickups. The hardware store and Kline's grocery still looked the same, but a medical clinic had been built between them. The house where Kevin Hartford once lived had been torn down, and in its place was a Mexican restaurant.

Dana had many regrets, and Kevin was one of them. On a blanket in the woods, he'd made all sorts of promises Dana realized later that he never intended to keep. He wanted out of the backwoods town as much as she did, and for a while, he made Dana believe he'd take her with him when he left. They talked about running away to the mountains, maybe out to the coast of California where no one could find them. There was no place in Dana's heart for Kevin, but she'd given up her virginity to him in hopes that he'd make good on his word that lasted as long as the act itself.

Alex had warned her about him, but Dana wasn't in a place where she could listen. Alex was preparing to go off to college, and Dana felt desperation closing in on her. She managed to make it through the rest of high school, but her graduation party was drinking a soda and toasting Barbier Point as it faded in the rearview mirror. Audrey, her mother, secretly helped her get set up in a small apartment in New Orleans since her father refused to help her "ruin her life" by snubbing college. Daniel Castilaw's financial support came with chains not strings. To further her education, Dana knew, meant that her father would continue to control every step she took.

"Mom, which way do I go?"

Dana realized they were sitting at the four-way stop in the middle of town. "Left."

Sydney turned onto a residential street. "Did we just see the whole thing?"

"Pretty much. There are bars and bait shops by the water, but you've just passed through the great metropolis of Barbier Point."

Sydney pursed her lips. "Would you consider going back home and living out of our car?"

"If push comes to shove, I'll buy a tent and we'll live at the campgrounds near the city where we can at least bathe," Dana said with a laugh.

Sydney was serious when she said, "We can make that work."

"Mind your speed through here. As I recall, the doughnut gestapo doesn't have much to do. You're gonna go a couple of miles, and the place will be on the right. I'll give you fair warning before we get there." Dana watched houses go by, trying to remember who had lived in them when she was young and wondering if anyone she'd known was still there. "The high school is right there on your left."

Sydney stared at the old brick building. "I'm glad you pointed it out, I might've missed it or at least confused it for the post office. How many kids were in your graduating class—two?"

"Oh, you are funny."

Dana inhaled deeply and let it out slowly in anticipation of seeing her father. Fourteen years was a long time, and she wondered if he'd changed. When she'd called him and explained her situation, the scathing lecture she expected had never come. "I have plenty of room," he'd simply said.

"Okay, Syd, slow way down, it's the next driveway to the right."

Sydney turned into the driveway and stopped. They both sat and stared at the house. The yard in front and around the home was huge and cut meticulously all the way to the marsh visible on either side. An old live oak was the centerpiece of the front lawn, some of its boughs touched the ground, and behind it sat the house with white columns along the front porch and balcony.

"Wow, this looks like a movie set. Is this a real plantation home?" Sydney asked.

"No, it was just designed to look kind of like one of those things. It's old, though."

As Sydney started slowly up the driveway, a squirrel scampered across the yard, and out of nowhere, a hawk swooped down and picked it up. She slammed on the brakes and stared open-mouthed. "Mom, what kind of place is this?"

"Apparently, not heaven for squirrels, poor little guy. There's a parking area behind the house. We never park on the circle drive." Dana imitated her father. "It detracts from the scenic beauty."

"Oh, faux faux, I'm sure our Subaru would be frowned

upon," Sydney quipped. "If anyone suggests I wear a hoop skirt, I'm running away."

"And I'll be right behind you. Pull up to the garage, I'm sure we'll be informed later where to more appropriately park," Dana said as they passed the large patio behind the house partially shaded by the rear balcony. She inhaled deeply, pulled the visor down, and gazed at her reflection. Her heavily highlighted hair needed a touchup, and her blue eyes looked as dull as she felt. Nervousness was apparent as a flush moved up her neck and crept across the pale skin of her face. Dana ran a hand through her shoulder-length hair and got out.

Daniel Castilaw ambled out onto the patio with the help of a cane. He was a tall thin man with a head of thick gray hair still carefully combed to minimize a prominent widow's peak. His face was clean shaven, and he looked dapper as always in a starched light blue collared shirt and a pair of navy slacks.

Dana swallowed hard as she gazed at him. During the years of their estrangement, he'd grown seemingly so old. She took Sydney by the hand and walked over to where he stood on the patio. "Hello, Dad, what's the deal with that?" She pointed at the cane, not knowing what else to say.

"Gout, it flares up from time to time, and arthritis." The hardness Dana remembered in his blue eyes was no longer there but seemed to be replaced with weariness. His gaze swept over her. "You look well," he said after clearing his throat. "And this must be Sydney."

"Yes, sir, nice to meet you."

Daniel smiled slightly as he regarded her. He put out his hand, and Sydney shook it. "Nice and firm, good eye contact, very well done," he said with a slight bow of his head. "You've grown into a fine young woman."

Sydney returned the smile. "Thank you."

Daniel turned when a woman stepped out of the back door. "Ladies, I'd like to introduce you to Clara Ford. She helps me around the house."

"It's a pleasure to meet you, Clara," Dana said.

Clara was an older lady but still appeared to be quite a few years Daniel's junior. Her short curly brown hair was held away from her face by a clip. She was short and stout. Clara straightened her white blouse as she walked over to Dana with a huge smile. "I'm so glad you're here," she said cheerily. "I've made lunch." She shook Dana's hand, then turned to Sydney. "So nice to meet you, young lady. I love your hat."

Sydney swept it off her head with her free hand. "I forgot I had it on," she said with a sheepish smile. "Very nice to meet you."

"Why don't y'all come inside and relax for a little while, then we'll get your things settled?" Clara suggested.

Dana glanced at her watch. "The movers will probably be here in the next hour or so."

Clara nodded. "We'll be ready for them."

The large kitchen looked much as Dana remembered it, except the old appliances had been replaced with the new stainless steel kind. Granite countertops had been installed, as well. The large bar that divided the cooking and seating areas was covered with dishes. Clara began moving them to the table as Daniel shuffled over to it and sat down.

"Sit, sit," Clara said as she busied herself.

"I'll be happy to help you." Dana reached for one of the glasses that had been set out, but Clara put a hand on her arm.

"Let me take care of this, darlin'. You take a seat, and catch up with your father. Lemonade, tea, or soda?"

"Tea for me," Dana said.

Clara quickly filled two glasses. "Take one of those to your father, please." She looked at Sydney in question.

"Lemonade, thank you."

Clara poured what looked like fresh-squeezed lemonade and handed it to Sydney, who followed her mother to the table and sat.

"Sydney, you'll be a senior in high school when you return after the summer, is that correct?"

"Yes, sir, and I don't play basketball or volleyball," she said with a smile. "I get asked that a lot because of my height."

"Do you play any sports?"

"I ride my skateboard. I like to water ski, too. I did that a lot last summer with one of my friends and her family."

"I'll bet Mike next door would love to hear that, he's always looking for an excuse to take his boat out," Clara offered as she joined them and began spooning gumbo into bowls.

"Mike Pride is still your neighbor?" Dana asked.

"Yes, Leona claims Mike is going through a late-life crisis. One week, he bought himself a new boat, and the next, a new truck. Unfortunately, his boat is for fishing, not skiing," Daniel said, meeting Sydney's eye. "Your mother's best friend, Alex, however, has that type of boat."

Dana nearly dropped her bowl when Clara passed it to her. "Alex? She's here?"

Daniel nodded. "She's been back going on three years now, she's a…"

"PA, a physician's assistant," Clara said. "She works up at the new clinic with Dr. Morris. Sweet woman, I take your father to see her on occasion."

Dana was elated. The last time she'd spoken with Alex was right before she married Troy. Alex had started a new job then, and the weekly calls that they'd enjoyed gradually dwindled to once a month. Sydney arrived not long after that, and Dana's time became limited. After a while, they lost touch altogether, but Dana had never stopped thinking about her.

"I know spring isn't gumbo weather, but Mike gave us a turkey at Christmas, and someone else did, too. We just didn't have any room in the freezer, so I decided to cook it." Clara set a bowl in front of Sydney. "Your father hasn't been happy with me, he's eaten his fill of it."

"Clara lives here," Daniel explained. "I don't get around like I used to. She's in the room down the hall from me, so the upper floor is yours to do with what you will."

"Thank you," Dana said gratefully. "We have quite a bit of furniture coming."

"Yes, your father told me." Clara finally settled into her chair and passed a basket of bread to Sydney. "I hired a few fellas to move everything into the attic. That way, you can set up your things and it'll feel more like home up there."

"I'm sorry you had to go to all that trouble," Dana said sincerely.

Clara smiled. "Oh, it wasn't a bother at all."

"What kind of work were you doing?" Daniel asked Dana as he picked up his spoon.

Dana tried not to stiffen. "I was managing a small store, kind of like a Hallmark shop, and the owner passed away. The heirs didn't want to continue running it, so they closed it and sold the building. I was Mr. Perrin's right hand. I took care of just about everything, so he paid me well. I was able to save for a rainy day, but when I was forced to take work that paid significantly less, I chipped right through my nest egg."

Dana was mindful of the advice her father had always given her about having a career in something that people would always need, like health care. She fully expected him to say that greeting cards and trinkets were not a wise course of action. She glanced at Sydney as Daniel sighed loudly.

"It's a tough world for small businesses. I expect that eventually one of those big drug chains will come in and run Murphy's pharmacy out. I'm sure you'll be able to find work here. It may not be along the lines of what you were doing, but with your experience, you'll be considered an asset. You could also take this time to go to school for something else if you'd like. Whatever you decide, you'll have a home here for as long as you want."

Dana couldn't even look at him she was so stunned. "Thank…you, Dad…that means a lot."

Chapter 2

"Go fish, Maw Maw."

"I think you're lyin'. I'll just bet you have a joker you're holding on to, Alexandra." Thelma drew a card and frowned at it. "I'm dying. It's not nice to take advantage of a woman on her last leg. You know my stools are white, that's a sure sign of death coming."

"You drink milk of magnesia like water, it's a wonder your urine isn't white," Alex Soileau said as she stared at her cards.

"My teeth are falling out. That means I'm at death's door."

"You had them pulled for dentures."

"Same thing. You mark my words, one day you're gonna be old like me, and you'll know how it feels."

"An asteroid could hit the earth, and after the years it would take for the dust to settle, you'd still be here rifling through the debris collecting bottles of booze and cigarettes."

"Disrespectful, that's what you are. I try to overlook it because your mother dropped you on your head when you were a baby, and your nut is probably cracked."

"She never dropped me. Do you have a king?"

"Nope, go fish. Two grown women playing a child's game, how silly."

"Well, what else do you want to do?"

"I want a drink and a cigarette," Thelma said pointedly as

she tossed her cards on the table. "I'm old and I'm dying, so I may as well go out feeling good."

Alex picked up the king and waved the card at her grandmother. "Who lied?"

"Did you hear me, Alexandra?"

"I did." Alex gathered the cards. "You're out of cigs and booze. You'll just have to wait until Mom gets back from the store."

"You could run right on up there to the Prop Stop and get me what I want. Won't take you but five minutes."

Alex looked at her watch. "Mom's been gone going on three hours, she'll be back any minute. You know I can't leave you alone. The last time I did, you drank all the cooking sherry and got a DUI because you took that scooter of yours out onto the road."

"Smug smart-ass little punk with a badge harassing a dying woman in a wheelchair. With all the crime going on out there, I should've kicked him right in the nuts. Had he gotten close enough, I would have and claimed it was a muscle spasm. Little dickhead."

Alex grinned. "Oh, I'm telling Momma you said bad words. Nice wig, by the way. The black suits you so much better than the reddish-brown. It does a better job of covering your horns, too."

"Shit, damn, hell, peckers, poo, I want a cigarette and a drink."

Alex scratched the back of her neck. "Peckers, poo, you are one foul-mouthed hussy."

Thelma stabbed a finger at her. "Now you're pissing me off, girl."

"You're always pissed off." Alex stood and put away the cards. "Momma's coming up the driveway. You'll be sucking on cigs and booze in no time."

A few minutes later, Jean walked in with an armload of bags. "Where the hell have you been?" Thelma bellowed.

"Don't bark at me, old woman. I had to wait on your

prescription at the pharmacy, then I had to go to the dollar store because Kline's didn't have the Little Debbie cakes your royal highness requires." Jean dropped her bags on the cooking island and raked a hand through her tousled blond pixie cut. "Dear God, it's so hot out there already." She pulled her wire-framed glasses from her face and held them up. "Look, the lenses steamed when I got out of the car."

"I'll get the rest of the groceries, Mom," Alex said as she passed Jean and walked outside.

The entire family had preached to Thelma about her copious use of booze and her pack-a-day habit. But Thelma was a grown woman with a somewhat sound mind, and it was her choice to peck away at her health, which was surprisingly good given her vices and the fact that she was significantly overweight. Alex's grandfather, Thelma's late husband, never drank, nor did he smoke. At sixty-nine, he was still jogging and happened to be doing that when he dropped dead of a sudden massive heart attack. So the point of Thelma taking care of her health by giving up harmful things was moot. Alex was fairly certain that her grandmother could eat a handful of nails, drink acid, set herself ablaze, and dive through a plate glass window and still be unscathed.

Alex grabbed a handful of bags, most of which were filled with Little Debbie treats, and headed for the back door, but before she could reach it, Thelma shot out. With a carton of cigarettes in her basket and a bottle of cheap wine in the drink holder of her electric scooter chair, she was on the move to her favorite spot on the patio. She ran over Alex's foot as though it was only a speed bump.

"Shit," Alex said with a groan.

The tires of the scooter skidded to a halt. Thelma threw it into reverse, causing Alex to jump out of her way. "Foul-mouthed hussy," she said with an evil grin and took off tooting the little horn next to the throttle.

"Enjoy your booze, Maw Maw, I hope it gives you gas," Alex called after her.

When Alex walked into the house, she found Jean stuffing boxes of cheap pastries on the lower shelf of the pantry so Thelma could reach them from her chair. "I know my heart is going to be broken when Momma finally passes away," Jean said. "But I'll tell you what, that pain ain't gonna last very long. What is she *dying* of today?"

"I have no idea, but she's claiming white stools," Alex said with a laugh as she helped Jean put away the groceries.

"Sarah and Margie just burst out laughing when I tell them about that old woman's antics, and I guess I'd laugh too if she wasn't my mother and I didn't have to put up with her twenty-four/seven. She's like a precocious ten-year-old that smokes and drinks." Jean pinched the skin of her forehead and closed her eyes. "I need to tell you something. It's right on the edge of my brain, and when I heard it, I thought, oh, my God, I can't wait to tell Alex."

"Was it about the Maggios getting a llama? That's all over town. From what I hear, Larry the llama has already escaped his confines twice, and the police responded to reports of a 'baby camel' headed south on Cypermort Street."

"No…" Jean continued to hold her forehead, then her eyes flew open. "Dana Castilaw is back in town and living with her father! That's it."

The muscles in Alex's stomach did a little flip-flop upon hearing Dana's name. "You don't say," she threw out casually as she put the milk in the refrigerator.

Jean returned to filling up the pantry. "Margie saw Clara at the grocery store. Clara was all excited and had her cart loaded to the brim with food. She told Margie that Dana had lost her job and fallen on hard times, so she and her daughter moved in with Daniel. I can't remember the girl's name, but I saw her at Audrey's funeral, adorable little thing with big brown eyes. Dana had just gone through her divorce, then Audrey died. That poor child looked terrible after facing those two blows back to back. You were in Shreveport then at PA school." Jean tapped her fingers on a box of cereal. "Her baby must've been two or three, so that would make her around...well, she'd be in her later teens. You should go by there and say hello. I imagine Dana needs a friend at this point."

Alex collected the empty bags. "She must've been flat broke to move back in with her father. Dana and Daniel didn't get along."

"He's a good man. He's suffered losses that would make the best of souls wither." Jean glanced at Alex. "I thought the news about Dana would thrill you, but you don't look excited."

"I am," Alex said nonchalantly. "Where did Maw Maw get the horn on her cart?"

Jean rolled her eyes. "Your father was cleaning out his shop and finally decided to give the old bikes he had stored in there to Goodwill. One of them had a horn. Momma got her hot little hands on it and duct taped it to her scooter. If she blows that thing at me again, you'll have to surgically remove it."

"I'm going to leave before that happens," Alex said as she headed for the door.

"What's the rush? What're you doing today?"

"All of the chores that build up while I'm working during the week."

Jean put a hand on her hip and shook a finger at Alex. "You need to get to work on finishing that treehouse of yours. Have you done anything with that kitchen since the last time I was over there?"

Alex grinned. "Why should I rush? You feed me so well over here."

"And you know I love it, but you should at least have a place where you can store food."

"I'll get right on that. See you this evening," Alex said as she walked out.

Thelma blew out a big plume of cigarette smoke as Alex passed her on the patio. "Where you goin', fake doctor?"

"Home, fake human."

Thelma threw back her head and laughed. "I do love you, jackass."

"Love you, too," Alex called over her shoulder, wishing she'd not decided to be healthy that morning and walk the mile to her parents' house. The walk back would provide her with time to think about the news her mother had to share. Alex felt like she had spent a lifetime purging Dana Castilaw from her mind, even though she'd always occupy her heart. But just the mention of Dana's name and the knowledge that she was in town made Alex feel that she was right back at square one.

They'd grown up together and were inseparable best friends. Dana with her wild imagination was always dreaming up games to play. Her favorite was house. Dana was the wife, Alex the husband. They'd go into the woods and pretend to be settlers, and Alex would build a shelter for them out of broken tree limbs and palmetto leaves. Dana would reward her with little kisses on the cheek. One day when Alex was eleven, Dana's kiss made her feel different. Alex realized she wanted more and not on the cheek. That revelation was only the beginning.

When girls in her class started talking about wanting to kiss boys, Alex knew she was the oddball because all she wanted to do was kiss Dana. As they grew, so did Alex's feelings, and they were the only secret she kept from her best friend. By the time she reached high school, Alex understood and accepted that she'd completely fallen in love with Dana. Their teen years were especially hard because it tore Alex's heart out to hear Dana show interest in a guy or hear her talk about wanting to be married to one.

Malcolm, Alex's oldest brother, had also fallen in love during high school and announced to the family over dinner one night that he intended to propose to this girlfriend. Alex never forgot that conversation. She remembered her father stating very clearly that love wasn't real when you're young. It was all an illusion driven by hormones. For Malcolm, that was true, but not for Alex.

Dana unknowingly broke her heart time and time again; going off to college had granted Alex a reprieve. When Dana called and told Alex she was getting married, Alex made up her mind to stop pining for a love she would never have, but her heart refused to get the message.

"The movers are about to start bringing up our things. Have you picked which room you want?" Dana asked as she reached the top of the stairs where Sydney stood.

"Which room was Aunt Mary's?"

"The one on the left at the end of the hall," Dana said with a slight smile.

"No disrespect, Mom, but I don't want that one. I never met her, but I feel like that one is still hers."

Dana nodded. "I understand. There's three more for you to choose from, so I need you to pick."

Sydney gazed at her thoughtfully. "Can I have your old room?"

"Yes, you can." Dana pointed to the door closest to the top of the stairs. "I'll take that one, and the room between us will be our living room. We'll put the couch and chairs in there."

Sydney folded her arms. "I don't remember how you said she died."

"She drank and she drove. Mary was a year younger than you, and at a party, she got really drunk, then got behind the wheel of a friend's car. This is why I harp on you all the time. She was a good girl but made several bad decisions one night. You read about it and see the stories on the news, but it's always someone else. It happens all the time, know what I mean?"

"Yes," Sydney said with a nod.

They both turned when the movers started up the stairs with Sydney's bed. Dana patted her on the shoulder. "Go show them where you want that set up."

Dana opened the door to what would be her room and looked around. A feeling of melancholy swept over her as she stared at the corner where her mother's sewing machine used to sit. Audrey loved to sew and make dresses for her daughters to wear, but she was terrible at it. When Mary and Dana were small, the uneven hems weren't that big of a deal, but as they grew older and became cognizant of the fact that one sleeve was often longer than the other, they shied away from their mother's designs. Dana closed her eyes, hearing echoes of laughter in her mind. It was the "girls room," where they got together with Audrey and talked about all sorts of things.

Mary's death changed everything. It brought Dana and her mother closer as they comforted each other in their grief. Daniel changed, too, and he was no longer the loving father she'd known. He was angry and demeaning in his attempts to control Dana. Audrey was caught in the middle and tried to explain that he was afraid he'd lose Dana, too, but that was little consolation to a teen who felt captive in her home. She'd mourned and missed her sister, but there were times that she was so angry at Mary for what she'd caused them all.

Alex had been her solace, the one person Dana could pour out her heart to and know she would be understood. With Alex, Dana felt part of something special, a bond that no one could ever break. They were like two halves of a whole that communed in a place known only to them.

Dana walked over to the window and stared at the old live oak with its massive boughs and remembered how she'd sneak into that same room and look for Alex in the shadows at night when she was not allowed to go out. Foolishly, Dana would go out onto the veranda, climb over onto a limb, and scurry down the tree like a squirrel. She and Alex would hike over to the wishing well, where they'd talk and toss coins and their dreams into the water. When Daniel finally caught Dana during one of her nocturnal escapes, he had the branches cut away from the house.

"Ma'am," one of the movers said as he poked his head into the room. "Where would you like your bed?"

"On this wall, facing the French doors, please."

Dana stepped into the hall and surveyed the mountain of boxes. She'd packed carefully and labeled them essential and nonessential. What they didn't have to use, like the kitchen items and a few other household things, would remain boxed and moved into Mary's old room. It would make moving out much easier when Dana was back on her feet financially.

Clara climbed the stairs, and when she got to the top, she let out a loud sigh and smiled. "How's it going up here?"

"Very well, thank you. I noticed that Mary's old room was empty. Do you think Dad would mind if we stored some things in there?"

"Oh, no, dear, I'm sure he won't. He hasn't been up here for years." Clara brushed at the beads of sweat forming on her forehead with the back of her hand. "I don't know if he told you or not, but he goes out with the boys every Saturday night, so he won't be here for dinner. So you just let me know what time you and Sydney would like to eat."

"Clara, you don't have to worry about us. This is your night off, you should prop up your feet or do something you enjoy."

Clara waved a hand. "Trust me, I relax plenty. This is probably the easiest job I've ever had. Sometimes, I feel guilty over receiving a paycheck. Before I began working for your father, I lived with my son and his wife and children." She smiled wistfully. "It was nice being around my grandbabies, but they're old enough that they don't need me looking after them. I just felt in the way there."

They stepped out of the way when two of the movers came up the stairs with Sydney's drawing table.

"I've worked since I was fourteen," Clara continued. "Like you, I found myself unemployed when the company I worked at for thirty years closed its office here. James, my son, was insistent that I move in with him, but I don't think his wife was ever truly happy with that idea. This job was a blessing because I'm still close to James and the kids, yet I have my own space."

Dana folded her arms and leaned a shoulder against the wall. "What's wrong with Dad health-wise?"

"He's just old. Arthritis makes it hard for him to get around, and he forgets things like when to take his blood pressure medicine. It was actually Alex who suggested that he bring someone in to look after him." Clara grinned. "Oh, he resisted that, but a nasty fall one day after he got light-headed was the wakeup call. So he hired me, and I keep up with his medication, make sure he eats, and I tend to things around the house that need to be done. You should know that I'm happiest when I'm busy. Sitting around idle too much is bad for someone my age. The mind starts to slip. I love to cook, and after cooking for myself for many years, it's a pleasure to have someone else to feed, so don't be shy about making requests."

Dana liked Clara, and she was thankful to have her around. Like her mother, Dana felt that Clara would be a good buffer between her and her father. And after seeing how much he had aged, it was comforting to know that he wouldn't be totally alone when she and Sydney could afford to go back to New Orleans.

"Is there anything we can do to make your life easier?" Dana asked.

"You are as sweet as Daniel said you would be, but don't you worry about me, I'm just fine. I'm gonna go back downstairs and make sure these moving men have plenty to drink. If you need anything at all, you just holler."

"Thank you." Dana watched as Clara slowly descended the stairs, her mind reeling from Clara's last comment. She wondered if Clara had lied just to make her feel better about being there because she could not fathom her father referring to her as sweet.

Chapter 3

The house was silent when Dana awoke the next morning. She walked out on the landing and listened for signs of life, unsure if anyone had arisen. Sometime after midnight, she'd gone into Sydney's room and asked her to save arranging her things until the daylight hours for fear that the banging and shuffling would awaken her father and Clara below.

She yawned as she strolled into the makeshift den in one of the bedrooms. A pang of homesickness besieged her as she stared at her sofa and chairs. She made a mental note to set up her coffeepot in the corner, so she could enjoy a cup in private. Sun streamed in through the French doors as she walked toward them. The creak they made when she opened them caused her to wince.

The May morning was cool as she stepped out onto the back veranda and watched the fog swirl through the grasses growing in the marsh. It was quickly burning off beneath the warmth of the sun that sparkled on the water in the distance. Dana saw herself enjoying mornings like this at the small bistro table and chairs that had been on her patio at the apartment. She made another mental note to find the set and bring it out there when the noise wouldn't bother anyone.

As she stood with her hands on the railing, she began to mentally assemble her to-do list. She would spend the day unpacking the things they needed and storing the rest. Then she would polish up her résumé, and come Monday morning, she would set out to find a job locally that would help her catch up on her bills. She also intended to continue to scour job listings in New Orleans and pursue anything she felt sustainable.

Her father's offer to help her go back to school sat way in the back of her mind. Her whole adult life had been about survival and providing for Sydney. She'd never had the option of continuing her education and had no idea what she wanted to do for a career if she had the choice. The sight of blood made her ill, so anything medical was out. Anything other than a few computer programs and surfing the Net confounded her, so programming school was not something she felt she could consider. Those were the only two things she could think of that would provide good money fresh out of school.

She walked over to the doors at Sydney's room and peered in. Sydney was sound asleep, flat on her stomach, lying diagonally across the bed as though she'd fallen there, her cellphone clutched in her hand. Her clothes had been put away; all the cups filled with pens were arranged on her drawing table. She'd set up her TV on a corner stand, and the shelves below it were filled with the DVDs she liked to watch. Dana groaned when she noticed that Sydney had tacked some of her favorite sketches to the wall. That would not go over well with her father if he ever did venture up there.

Dana turned as she heard the back door open below. As she walked back over to the railing and looked down, she spotted Clara dropping a bag of trash into the large receptacle by the garage. Dana scampered back inside her room, put on a bra, pulled her T-shirt on, and went in search of coffee.

Clara was busy making biscuits when Dana walked into the kitchen. The smell of fresh-brewed coffee drew her to the pot. "Good morning. Did we keep y'all awake with all the bustling around up there last night?"

"I didn't hear a thing. This old house is as solid as a rock. Your father sleeps with plugs in his ears because every little sound causes him to stir. I nearly drove him crazy when I first moved in because I get up to go to the bathroom a lot during the night. If you made noise, I'm certain he didn't notice." Clara slid a pan into the oven. "I just want you to know I don't normally make such elaborate breakfasts except on Sunday mornings, but I certainly will if you and Sydney want something besides cereal each day."

Dana chuckled as she filled her coffee cup. "Clara, you're going to spoil us rotten if I don't watch it."

"She'll change the sheets on your bed before you have a chance to get out of it," Daniel said as he walked into the kitchen. "If I were a smaller man, I'm certain I'd find myself in the washer."

"Good morning, Dad. Did you have a good time last night?" Dana asked.

"I did, yes. Do you remember Nate Spearman?" He slowly took a seat at the table.

Dana studied her father's clean-shaven face as she thought. "Was he the one that had the seafood shop out near the boat launch?"

Daniel nodded. "He discovered a talent for the guitar some time back and plays bluegrass music with a few of the men in town. He comes out here and picks me up every weekend and takes me to watch them play at The Spinnaker."

Dana cocked her head. "I didn't know you liked that kind of music."

"I don't, it sounds like caterwauling to me, but it is nice to escape Clara's doting for a little while."

Clara chuckled and glanced at Dana. "He means that."

"And yet I'm grateful for all you do for me." Daniel nodded. "That was my weekly expression of gratitude, please make a note of it."

The tired expression on his face changed as Sydney walked into the kitchen. Dana recognized the affection in his gaze; she'd seen it often when it was bestowed upon her. That was before they lost Mary and the light in his eyes had gone out.

"Good morning, Sydney. Are you all settled in?"

"Yes, sir," she said with a sleepy smile, her hair a mess from being slept on while it was still wet from her shower.

"Very good. Would you like to take a walk with me after breakfast?"

Sydney nodded. "Sure, Grandpa."

Dana felt her brow rise when her father genuinely smiled. That was something she hadn't seen in a very long time.

Dana helped Clara clean the kitchen after breakfast and took Sydney's plate when she finished eating. She was a little nervous about the walk Daniel had suggested. He obviously wanted to spend some alone time with Sydney, and Dana hoped he wouldn't say anything hurtful that would make Sydney uncomfortable with living there.

"Are you ready to walk, Grandpa?" Sydney asked as she stood and stretched.

"I am."

Dana watched as her father stood slowly and began to shuffle toward the back door. She wondered how they'd walk anywhere. "Y'all have a nice time." She watched as Sydney opened the door and held it for Daniel.

Once they were outside, Daniel reached into his pocket and pulled out a small set of keys. "Young lady, if you'll go into the garage through that door over there, you'll find a switch on the wall to your right just as you go in. The light will come on, and the big door will open." He held out the keys to Sydney. "One of these will start the golf cart. Drive it on out here and pick me up, if you would, please."

"Okay, cool." Sydney did as Daniel instructed and found the cart parked next to a pickup. The cart zipped as she stepped on the accelerator, and she drove out of the garage. "Um… Grandpa, it may take me a few tries before I can take off smoothly."

"And here I am without my helmet." Daniel climbed onto the seat with her and laid his cane across his lap. "Drive us around the other side of the garage."

Sydney's takeoff was a bit jerky. She glanced at Daniel and said, "Sorry."

"You're doing fine. Just take us along the marsh but not too close. Clara misjudged one day, and our ride ended abruptly. It took me hours to clean all the mud out of this cart. So tell me about your hobbies."

"I like to ride my skateboard, sketch, and film things. I want to go to cinema photography school when I graduate. My dream is to work on TV or movie sets."

Daniel gazed at her for a moment. "I used to tell your mother to always work in a profession that people will need, and she'd always have a job. One does need to escape the reality of life on occasion either through books or movies, so I would say cinema photography would fall into that category."

"I need to find a job right now because I want to help Mom, and I really want a new video camera."

"There are a few places in town that could use someone your age. I'm sad to say there probably won't be any filming involved, likely stocking of shelves or burger flipping," Daniel said as he gazed out at the marsh.

"As long as it comes with a paycheck, I'll take it. What kind of work do you do?"

"I was an attorney like my father was. I always believed that your mother would've been a good lawyer. She's a woman of her convictions, and she could argue the mortar out of a brick wall."

Sydney's chuckle grew into a laugh. "You got that right."

"No matter how many times her mother and I punished her for playing in the marsh, Dana would go right back in the first chance she got. There was always a pet turtle or frog. I'd come home in the evenings, and sometimes, your grandmother would be completely frazzled because Dana had smuggled some sort of creature up to her room. One time, it was an injured duck. We had that thing for years. Would you like to guess what she named him?"

"Donald?"

"Albert." Daniel gazed at Sydney with a smile as she laughed. "On occasion when I come out here, I see birds, sometimes a snake or an alliga—" Daniel grabbed the canopy support when Sydney slammed on the brakes.

"You see what?" she asked, eyes wide.

"They can't harm us, we're in the cart," Daniel said with confidence.

"It has no doors. Whatever is out there can get in here with us."

"I've been out here hundreds of times, and nothing of the sort has ever happened."

"When I use that argument with Mom, she tells me 'that don't mean it won't.'"

Daniel chuckled. "She's a very wise woman. Turn us around and head back to the garage. I'd like to show you something."

"Okay."

Daniel held on to the support of the canopy again as Sydney made a sharp turn. "How will you get to work when you find a job?"

"Mom will have to take me, or if she's not using the car, I'll drive it."

"Are you a good driver?"

Sydney nodded with a grin. "Don't hold my driving right now against me."

"Do you know how to drive a stick?"

Sydney shrugged. "I've ridden a few brooms, but they don't go very far."

Daniel laughed. "Oh, you've made a joke, how cute. Sarcasm is a sign of intelligence."

Sydney wheeled into the garage and stopped. She took the keys from the ignition of the cart and handed them to Daniel. "Thanks for letting me drive, Grandpa."

"And thank you for not going off into the marsh." He pointed at a dark blue truck covered in a light dust. "This is a Nissan Frontier, it has air and heat, but a manual transmission. If you can learn how to drive it, it'll be yours."

"Dad!"

Daniel and Sydney turned to find Dana standing in the doorway of the garage looking stunned. "That's a very generous offer, but we can't accept it."

Eyes full of truck lust, Sydney asked, "Why not?"

"I can't afford to insure it right now, honey."

"Sydney, would you give us a moment alone, please?" Daniel asked.

"Yes, sir," she said as she walked past Dana, eyeing her warily.

Dana waited until Sydney went into the house before she spoke. "I need you to talk to me before you do things like this."

"She's my granddaughter and nearly grown. I've missed out on a lot, so you'll have to forgive me if I want to do something special for her. Look at this." Daniel wiped a hand across the hood and held it up. Dust covered his palm. "I haven't been able to drive in over a year, this truck is going to waste. I'm not even sure the battery still has a charge."

"Then sell it and get your money out of it."

"I don't need money," Daniel said, raising his voice. "I need..." He scrubbed his face in frustration. "It's a gift. Please allow me to give it to Sydney. Insurance isn't a problem. I'll be more than happy to take care of that."

Dana's shoulders sagged. "Can I have a little time to think about this?"

Daniel nodded. "Take all the time you need," he said as he shuffled past her.

"To the left! I said left, Alex! Damn it!"

Alex killed the engine to the tractor and threw up her hands. "I can't hear a thing you're saying, Captain Mumbles. You have to scream over the sound of the engine."

"You don't just kill a machine like that, you throttle down," Wade Soileau exclaimed. "You went to school for almost a decade, and you don't know your right from your left."

Thelma, who had parked her scooter nearby, threw back her head and laughed.

Alex shot her a look, then turned to her father. "You were pointing to the right!"

"I want this log right here. Set it atop the others." He threw up his hands. "It's a cabin, Alex. You played with Lincoln Logs as a kid, you know how to build one."

Alex had grown tired of being yelled at. First, there was the toolbox she plowed over because Wade had left it in the middle of the yard, then she picked up the wrong log, even though she'd been instructed to do so. She loved working with her dad on his goofy projects, but the whole log cabin idea was foolish in her opinion, though she understood the logic. Thelma could wheel her scooter into his shop, and it was no longer a man cave. The cabin he was building would only have a two-foot-wide door in which to access it. It was also on the far corner of the property, but Thelma had already proven she and her scooter could handle rough terrain.

"Dad, I can push trash with this thing, but I'm not the person you need for the precise movements this job calls for," Alex said, hoping that he'd let her off the hook and she could go home and enjoy her day off.

"Well, I don't want you on this end. I could drop a log on you."

"Wasting all that gas and time when you could be back up at the house taking care of poor little Bert," Thelma said as she shook her cigarette at Wade. "Alex, you be thankful you don't like men because this is what they do. They eat the food you cook, they sleep in the bed you make, and they spend the rest of their time doing stupid shit like this."

If there was one thing Thelma enjoyed, it was tormenting everyone else. She chastised Alex and Wade for failing to do enough for Jean, but then she turned right around and made her daughter feel as though she could never do enough for her. Wade was her absolute favorite target because she could get under his skin much more easily than Jean and Alex. And when she was really in the mood to piss them all off, she referred to Jean as Bert and Wade as Ernie because Jean was tall and thin, and Wade was shorter and stocky. A fan of the Muppets, Thelma dubbed Alex Kermit, but if anyone made the mistake of calling Thelma Miss Piggy, her reaction was similar to an atomic bomb going off.

Wade put his hands on his hips and glared at her. "Go on back to the house, Thelma, and leave us alone. Take the new trail I made, it ain't as muddy."

"I've been down that trail, and it don't lead back to the house. It goes right off into the swamp!"

"That's right," Wade said with a grin. He turned back to Alex. "I want you to lift the log and set it to my left."

Alex blew out a breath. "But you were pointing to the right."

"Then move it to the right," Wade exploded.

"Stop yelling at me, Dad. I could be mowing my own grass, or better yet, lying on the couch."

Wade tore off his tattered cowboy hat and raked a handkerchief across his bald head. "I'm sorry, I just want to get as much done as I can before the rain starts up again." He pointed to the spot where he wanted the log. "Would you put it there, please?"

Alex fired up the tractor again and slowly moved the log connected to a chain. Wade motioned for her to lower it while he pushed it into position. Then he began unfastening the chain. It was a long arduous task, her lifting a log, him hooking it up, moving it into position, then waiting for him to set it. Her mind began to wander.

"What'd you wish for?"

Alex strained her eyes to see Dana in the pale moonlight. "You know I can't tell you."

"You mean you won't. You know telling them won't make any difference. If a wish does come true, it's just coincidence." Dana moved close to Alex and took her hand. They began

walking the trail that led to where Alex had parked her car. Beams of moonlight found their way through the thick foliage and landed on Dana's head and back as she walked ahead in the shadows, her hand behind her still grasping Alex's. "Is it a different wish each time?"

"No, always the same."

Dana stopped walking and turned so that they were face to face. "So it never comes true because you ask for it all the time. Tell me your secret."

Alex could feel Dana's breath on her skin, the warmth of her body so close. "I know throwing money in that stinking well won't make wishes come true, especially mine. I just like to pretend and hope that maybe I'm wrong, so I won't tell." She flinched when Dana's nose brushed against her neck.

"What perfume is that?"

"Umm...musk...I think. It comes in the bottle with the orange lid."

"You always wear it, and when I hug you, my clothes smell like it." Dana wrapped her arms around Alex's waist, her nose still pressed against her neck. "I could just stand here and sniff it all night."

Alex closed her eyes, wishing she would. She was completely under love's sweet spell, and it compelled her to tilt her head slightly. Her mouth was inches from Dana's when she realized what she was about to do. Alex stepped back abruptly. "I think I hear Old Man Wicker."

"Shit," Dana whispered and took off running toward the car.

Alex jumped when a glove hit her in the chest.

"You been in Thelma's wine?" Wade asked as he stared up at her.

Chapter 4

Clint Beaudreaux stared at Dana's résumé. "Do you know anything about seafood?"

"I love to eat it," Dana said with a smile. "I'll be honest with you. I don't know anything about logistics, but I'm certain that I can learn."

Clint's chair creaked as he sat back. "It's fairly simple, but it's important. I need someone responsible in that position, that's why I'm considering you over the younger applicants applying for the job. I can't start you out at what you were making before, though."

Dana nodded. "I understand."

"We do pay fifty percent of employee health insurance, and I feel like we have a pretty good plan. Not many businesses in town offer that anymore. It's a casual workplace, you can wear jeans. I'm a pretty laid-back boss as long as the job is getting done right. This position is Monday through Friday, so you'd have your evenings and weekends with your daughter. Does any of this compensate for the cut in salary that you're used to?"

"It does, and I'm interested in the position if you're willing to give me a shot." Dana hoped that Clint didn't notice the sweat beading on her upper lip. She'd not seen much in Barbier Point that paid more than minimum wage. The position of logistical coordinator for Beaudreaux's Seafood was the only job that would put her remotely close to the money she needed to make.

Clint stared at her as he tapped his index finger on his desk. "I'm about sick of people coming in late and calling off for hangovers. Is punctuality a problem for you?"

"I take my work seriously. I'm rarely sick, and I do know how to set an alarm clock," Dana said with a smile.

Clint stood and put out his hand. "Then welcome to Beaudreaux's Seafood."

Dana shook it with a relieved sigh. "Thank you for the opportunity, Clint."

"You're dressed nice, so I'm not going to take you out back, but I will show you your office." Clint led her into the hallway and up a flight of stairs. The room he led her into had a low ceiling, and the desk was built into a wall of windows that overlooked the bays below. A woman sat there on the phone as she pecked at a computer keyboard. She looked like a DJ wearing a headset with a mic in front of her.

"This is my wife, Lisa. I'll introduce you when she wraps up her conversation," Clint said.

Dana estimated Clint to be in his mid- to late forties; his goatee was still dark but had a fair amount of gray in it. Salt-and-pepper hair poked out from beneath the cap he wore, and his tanned face had its share of lines from age and being in the sun. His wife, however, appeared to be in her early thirties. Her thick dark hair was cut in a short bob with the longer sides tucked behind her ears. She was short and petite but had breasts that looked as though they'd pop out of her pink scoop-neck T-shirt at any second.

"We call this the hawk's nest because you can see everything happening below," Clint explained. "Crews clean up the catch, then they load it into storage or refrigerated trucks and haul the product to our buyers. We have to work closely with Mother Nature, and sometimes, she really makes our job difficult. We may have a customer waiting on a ton of shrimp." Clint held up a hand. "That's figuratively speaking and a fantasy on my part, but the haul from the boats that day might be light. So you're gonna have to make decisions if you should hold the catch for a day and wait for more before you ship a half load. It depends on what the weather will be like the following day and how bad the customer needs the product. We only ship half loads if our back is against the wall because the fuel costs cut deeply into profits. Your eyes are glazing over."

Dana blinked and shook her head. "I'm just taking it all in."

Clint smiled. "You're nervous, that's a good sign. The ones who shrug like it's no big deal scare the crap out of me."

Dana swallowed hard, wishing she had the nerve to ask what the turnover rate for this position was.

When Lisa hung up the phone, she turned in her chair and smiled up at Dana. Clint put a hand on her shoulder. "Baby, this is Dana Castilaw. She's the woman you're going to be training for this job."

Lisa sprang out of the chair like a kangaroo and threw her arms around Dana's neck. "I'm so happy to meet you."

"Honey, this is inappropriate," Clint said as he pried Lisa off Dana. His face held a flush as he smiled sheepishly. "Lisa prefers to be outside managing the loading dock."

Lisa threw up both hands. "Oh! It's not a bad job. It's like being in a treehouse, woohoo, ya know? When're you starting?"

Clint scratched the back of his neck. "We didn't discuss that. When can you start?"

"Tomorrow?" Dana said with a shrug.

Clint stopped Lisa when she lunged for Dana again in her excitement. "That's great," he said. "Thursday and Friday, we can go through all the paperwork and give you a good overview, and by Monday, you'll be ready for full-on training."

As Dana turned into the driveway of the house that afternoon, she could see her father sitting in the shaded side yard in an Adirondack chair, a book in his hands. She knew she needed to talk to him about the truck but was grappling with the real reason she didn't want to accept it—pride. A second vehicle would come in handy since Sydney had snagged a job on her first day of searching. But to have her father pay for the insurance made Dana feel even more beholden to him than she already did.

She was feeling a bit overwhelmed about the job she'd just committed herself to. It appeared to be more stressful than Clint had implied, and again, pride reared its ugly head. If she could not handle the position, her father would know she failed, and that was reprehensible to her. So when she no sooner had climbed out of the car and Sydney hit her with the latest barrage of reasons she should have the truck, a lit match was set to Dana's fuse.

"Mrs. Susan told me I could work breakfast, lunch, and dinner shifts at the diner. With those kinds of hours and tips, I could make enough to pay for the insurance and help you. But I need wheels, Mom. I could've been on the schedule today, but you had the car, and when you get a job, I'm really gonna be screwed—"

"Stop! I just got here and you're already in my face, Sydney." Dana put a hand to her forehead. "Just let me breathe for a minute."

"Sorry, I was excited," Sydney said as she backed away.

Dana hated that she'd hurt Sydney's feelings, but she was a little too riled to apologize before Sydney went back into the house. She turned and looked at her father; he was sitting straight up staring at her. Dana huffed as she tossed her purse on the hood of her car and walked over to his little oasis in the shade.

"You ought not yell at that child," Daniel said as he closed his book.

"You never had any problem doing that to me," Dana retorted hotly as she sat in the chair next to him.

"Did you get the job?"

"I did." Dana blew out a breath. "Your offer of the truck is very kind, and it has come at the right time. If you could cover the insurance for now, I will pay you back when I start getting paid. It may take me a little while to pay the whole premium. I do have some bills I need to take care of right away. When Sydney starts making regular money, she needs to pay you on the truck, as well. She'll take better care of it if she's paying a note."

Daniel took the book that was sitting in his lap and laid it on the table next to his chair. He stared at the marsh as he said, "There are times that I think about throwing Molotov cocktails through the windows of this house and just sitting back as it burns to the ground. The only thing that keeps me from doing it is the knowledge that it will someday be yours."

Dana stared at the side of his face, trying to decide how to process his comment. The house had been the pride of the Castilaw family for generations. "Why would you consider that?"

"It's a thing, and in my old age, I'm tired of being owned by things. It holds memories that can't be released by opening the windows or rearranging the furniture. Bitterness has seeped into the foundation. When I'm gone and if you have the opportunity to sell it, do so without compunction." He sighed, grabbed his cane, and stood slowly. "The mistakes I've made can't be undone, but you can decide not to follow in my footsteps," he said as he slowly ambled away.

"What does that mean, Dad?"

Daniel didn't answer, nor did he look back. Dana watched him go and sank back into her chair. She supposed that was as close to an apology that she would ever get from him. Perhaps making her feel imprisoned at times was his way of expressing his love for her. As a parent, if Dana had two children and lost one, she felt a day wouldn't go by without expressing her adoration for the one she had left. It was hard for her to understand that the affection she'd once known from her dad suddenly vanished when Mary did. She often wondered if maybe he'd wished it had been her who was killed instead of her sister.

Dana got up and went into the house where she found

Sydney sitting at her drawing desk doodling on a pad. "I'm sorry. I was feeling a little overwhelmed about my new job when I got home," she said as she took a seat on Sydney's bed.

Sydney gazed at her. "Congratulations."

"Thanks, baby. Let's talk about the truck."

Sydney's facial expression conveyed that what she was about to hear next wasn't going to be good news.

"I told your grandfather that you need to pay for the truck, so you need to get with him and decide on an amount. Until you get proficient at driving it, you'll have to drive my car to work and I'll drive your truck."

"Yes!" Sydney exclaimed as she pounded on the table. "Thanks, Mom! I'm gonna go talk to Grandpa right now!"

Before Dana could say anything else, Sydney ran from the room.

"Dr. Soileau, I have a message for you."

Alex clamped her lips together tightly and tried to smile at the new receptionist. "It's not Soileww it's pronounced like the bird, swallow—not Alex swallows, just Soileau. And I'm not a doctor, I'm a PA, so Alex will do just fine."

Kimmie, Cammy, Sammy whoever handed her a piece of paper. "Got it."

Alex stuffed the message into her pocket because she was sure it was from her mother on behalf of Thelma, who was dying of something new and wanted "the good drugs." She inhaled deeply, breathed out, and opened the exam room door. "Good afternoon, Mrs. Hurst," Alex said as she walked into the exam room. "How're you today?"

"Rotten."

"What's the trouble?" Alex said, looking at the chart. The reason for the visit was marked "consult."

"My new insurance doesn't work with my gynecologist, so I had to get another one, and he's all the way out in Houma. I have an appointment, but it'll be almost a month before I can get in to see him because I need to be put on hormones. Yesterday, I assaulted my husband with a tomato, and an hour later, I couldn't remember what he did to make me so mad. For the first time in my life, I look like a Barbie doll but just between the legs. My vagina is gone. Poof, it's missing. The only reason I'm not having a hot flash is because I'm sitting directly under your air-conditioning vent. I haven't had a full night's sleep in over a month. So what I need is an antidepressant to keep me sane until I can get in to see my other doctor. This is a public service on your part because if I don't get something to level out my mood, I'm gonna go on a rampage. I'm not a violent woman, I don't know how to shoot a gun, but I do wield a mean tomato, and I will shit on your doorstep. Now do you understand how serious I am at this moment?"

Alex was still stuck on the mental image of the Barbie but nodded. She looked at the chart and said, "I see here that you've taken Zoloft before. How did that work for you?"

Mrs. Hurst stared at the ceiling as she thought. "You put me on that after my mother died and I was having a hard time coping. I was able to catch myself before I slapped the shit out of someone, so I'd say it worked fine."

Alex looked over the vitals and was pleased with what she saw. "Just let me do a routine assessment, and I'll take care of that prescription for you. When was your last period?"

Mrs. Hurst pursed her lips and looked up at the ceiling again. "I'd say November."

Alex made a notation on the chart, then pulled her stethoscope from around her neck. "Some antidepressants work very well with relieving menopausal symptoms, not just the emotional and mental ones. You may find you won't need hormone therapy."

"Will my vagina come back?"

Alex smiled as she listened to Mrs. Hurst's lung sounds. "I don't believe so, but there are creams—"

"Whew, I'm flashing."

"Yes, you are." Alex watched her face turn dark red. She picked up the chart and fanned her with it.

Mrs. Hurst wiped her face with the back of her hand. "Do you smell cookies?"

Alex sniffed. "No, I don't."

"I smell cookies all the time, and I crave sweets. Last night, I served cake for dinner, that's how the milk got into the pantry. I didn't find it until this morning, and of course, it was ruined. You see, that's a problem, too. I can't focus, and I forget...do you smell cookies?"

Alex finished her exam and escorted Mrs. Hurst back to the front desk. While her patient checked out, Alex wrote up the script and made final notations on the chart, which she handed to the clerk. "I hope you feel better, but if you don't or if you have any problems, come back and see me."

"Your mom called," the receptionist said as she handed Alex a slip of paper.

"Thanks," Alex said distractedly as she read: *Dana called the house looking for you, this is her number...* Alex tucked it into her pocket as the muscles in her stomach contracted. She was torn between wanting to see Dana again and avoiding her.

She returned to the exam rooms and pulled the next chart. "Good afternoon, Mr. Mayeau, how are you today?"

"Horrible. I feel like I have glass in my pecker."

Alex sighed internally. Apparently, the rest of her day was going to be filled with missing vaginas and broken peckers.

Chapter 5

"Don't get frustrated. It's not easy getting used to a clutch, but once you get the hang of it, it'll all feel natural." Dana gripped the door handle. "Okay, try again. Ease off and press evenly on the accelerator at the same time." The truck lurched forward and died. Sydney laid her head against the steering wheel. "Hey, we're getting somewhere, you jumped at least two feet. We should make it home in time for dinner tomorrow night."

"You stopped being funny an hour ago."

"Baby, did you expect to master this in an hour?"

Sydney sat straight up. "Yes, and I'm gonna do it." She turned the key, pressed the accelerator, and let off the clutch. The truck lurched again, but this time, she managed to give it enough gas to keep it going.

"Good, very good. Now push in the clutch and shift into second."

Sydney made that transition smoothly. "I did it!"

"Now stop." Sydney shifted into neutral and brought the truck to a halt. "Great job." Dana patted her on the shoulder. "Downshifting will be the last lesson. Keep practicing your starts because that is the hardest part. So hop us back to the house."

Sydney glared at her. "Stop making fun of me."

"I'm not."

"It feels like it."

Dana shrugged. "I'm trying to be cute to take your mind off your frustration."

"It's not working."

Sydney managed to take off again, though it wasn't smooth. "Can I say, 'yay, good job'?"

"I'd rather you didn't." Sydney stared at the road. "I'm trying to focus."

"Okay, I'll just sit over here and be... Stop!"

Sydney slammed on the brakes, and the truck skidded to a halt, then promptly died. She looked furious as she stared at Dana. "Did you just make me lock 'em up for a turtle?"

"I didn't know if you saw it or not."

"Mom, all you had to say was, 'Hey, there's a turtle, don't hit it.'"

"Well, I wanted to get it out of the road before anyone else came along." Dana opened her door and hopped out.

"You're driving me crazy," Sydney said lowly as she listened to her mom sweet talk the hapless creature in the middle of the road. Dana bent down and grasped either side of the shell, then suddenly hiked it like a football. Sydney stared at her open-mouthed as she dashed back to the truck.

"You threw a turtle, Mom. What's wrong with you?"

Dana's eyes were wide as she slammed the door. "It hissed at me like a cat, and it had claws like one!"

"Folks 'round here would call that a snapper," Sydney said with a strong country accent. "Some might even call it dinner."

"Speaking of, let's go home."

Sydney's next start went smoother. "Grandpa said you used to catch turtles and frogs all the time, and you had a duck named Albert."

Dana released a sigh. "That wasn't me, it was Mary. Take a left up ahead if you feel comfortable enough driving where there will probably be more cars."

Sydney glanced at her. "You okay?"

"Yeah," Dana said with a weak smile as she wondered if Daniel's memory was simply failing or if there were times he actually thought she was Mary.

Sydney managed to make it back to the house without stalling out. A sporty-looking convertible was parked at the top of the circle drive. "Your grandpa must have company," Dana said as she climbed out, but when they walked toward the back door, she noticed her father in his chair beneath the trees with a book in hand.

"There they are," Clara chirped happily as they walked inside.

Dana stopped in her tracks as elation swept through her. Alex rose from the chair where she'd been seated. It seemed the only thing that had changed about her was the length of her hair. It no longer cascaded down her back and over her shoulders in dark waves. It was cut in long wispy layers and hung just past her jaw and seemed to accentuate the mouth that Dana always envied. The dip in Alex's top lip, which Dana's mother had always referred to as Cupid's bow, was very pronounced. What came naturally for Alex, most women attempted to draw with pencils and lipstick. Her heavily lidded eyes and dark lashes still had that sexy smoldering look that at one time caused every boy in town to chase her.

"You're still beautiful. I hate you, I love you, I have missed you!" Dana said as she raced into Alex's arms.

Alex gently pushed Dana away and looked her over with a smile. "You're all grown up and much prettier than I remembered." She rolled her eyes when Dana fingered a lock of her hair. "And still touchy-feely."

Dana laughed and pulled Sydney close. "Alex, this is my daughter, Sydney."

Alex smiled warmly as she put out her hand. "It is so great to finally meet you."

"You too," Sydney said as she shook Alex's hand.

Dana put her hand on Sydney's shoulder. "Alex is my oldest and dearest friend. She and I used to get into all kinds of trouble, and she *isn't* going to tell you anything about those days."

Alex winked at Sydney. "She hopes."

"Dana, convince Alex that she needs to stay for dinner," Clara said as she set a dish on the table.

"Oh, yeah, you have to stay," Dana agreed.

Alex looked uncomfortable. "I feel bad enough about dropping in without calling first. My plan was just to say hello and see if you'd like to get together some time."

Clara completely ignored her. "What would you like to drink, dear? We have lemonade, tea, and soda."

"As I recall," Dana began with a smile, "she likes to mix tea and lemonade." Dana hugged Alex again. "Please stay. I'd love to sit out on the front porch with you again like we used to."

"I heard her say yes." Clara turned to Sydney. "Didn't you hear Alex say yes?"

Sydney nodded. "I'm pretty sure I did."

"Why are you ganging up on Alex?" Daniel asked as he slowly made his way into the kitchen.

"We want her to stay for dinner," Clara said.

Daniel nodded. "She must."

Dana poured half a glass with lemonade, then filled it the rest of the way with tea. She set it with a grin at the place setting next to hers. "Sit."

Alex cocked a brow as she pulled out a chair. "Still bossy."

"You don't know the half of it," Sydney said as she took a seat across from her.

Alex smiled. "You and I will have to talk later." She then set her gaze on Daniel. "How're you feeling?"

"I'm doing just fine." Daniel pointed to the glass of water that Clara had just set in front of him. "I drink this all day long. Even if I didn't take your advice, Clara would give me no choice. Now let's leave work back at the office, and you tell me how your folks are doing."

"They're fine. It's been a few years, but Dad is still adjusting to retirement. He gets up at the same time each morning, dresses, and meets Richard and Ken at the same gas station where they used to meet and carpool to the plant. They have coffee in the shop there and talk, then he comes home and starts projects that irritate Mom. She's still taking care of Maw Maw."

Daniel revealed a hint of a smile. "How is Thelma?"

"She's…Thelma," Alex said with a smile.

"Tell us the storm story," Dana said as she passed Alex a bowl of potatoes. She glanced at Clara. "Have you heard it?"

"I don't believe I have."

Dana laughed. "You have to tell it, Alex."

Alex sighed and gazed at Sydney. "I don't remember what hurricane it was, but we had to evacuate. My grandparents weren't living with us then, and they had a place just outside of Baton Rouge. We packed up and went to stay with them until the storm passed. My dad's brother went with us, and during the drive, Dad warned Uncle Eric all about Maw Maw, who is my mother's mother. So we get there, and I'm sure my uncle was expecting a two-headed monster. Maw Maw was on her best behavior, and Uncle Eric thought that Dad was just messing with him.

"The storm actually missed Barbier Point and went straight through Baton Rouge. As the weather grew bad, so did Maw Maw. She started drinking and smoking like a fiend. Every meal she cooked had cigarette ashes in it. When a gust of wind would hit the house, she'd start screaming that we were all going to die. She made me and my brothers wear life jackets. All of this was going on, and we still had power. But when the storm really started to set in, it was in the middle of the night, and we were all sleeping. Of course, the electricity goes out, and she starts screaming, 'Everyone, get up, we have lost power, get up.' Then she went outside and got the flare gun out of my granddad's boat and shot the roof off the garage."

Dana covered her mouth as she laughed. "She nearly burned the house down."

Sydney shook her head. "I don't understand. Why would she shoot a flare gun?"

"We all wondered the same thing, but she said she did it to warn the neighbors that the power had gone out. My maw maw is kind of crazy," Alex said with a laugh. "We don't understand half the things she does. But after that storm, my uncle told us that if there was another hurricane, he'd rather stay put and face it than spend it with my maw maw."

Dana watched as Alex blew on her coffee to cool it. "I'm sorry if dinner felt awkward. I noticed that you tried to include Dad in some of the conversations."

"He doesn't talk very much when he comes to see me at the office. Clara usually joins us in the exam room and tells me what's been going on with him."

"He's been acting very strange."

Alex gazed at Dana with concern. "How so?"

"Dad's been nice. He's been smiling, and he gave Sydney his truck and offered to pay the insurance on it. He told Clara that I was sweet." Dana shook her head. "So weird."

Alex leaned her head against the back of the chair and smiled. "Maybe he's trying to make amends."

"I sense that's he's trying. He hasn't lectured me once or berated me for the loss of my job. He's actually been very gracious. It throws me off balance because I don't know where to step with him. We haven't even been here a full week, and sometimes, I feel like he's waiting for me to get really settled in and comfortable before he picks me apart. I don't want to talk about him, though. I want to hear about you."

"I'm glad you're sitting down because I think you're gonna freak when I say I bought the old place with the wishing well."

Dana's eyes went wide. "You're kidding me."

"Nope, now you can come over and toss your pennies

without having to worry about Old Man Wicker running you off with his shotgun. When he died, Oliver used it for a camp. He took decent care of it, but when I bought it, the place had not been updated since Wicker died. I've basically had to gut it room by room."

"I wanna see it," Dana said, eyes alight. "I always wondered what it looked like inside. I remember that it was always covered in vines and stuff. Being on stilts, it looked like a treehouse."

"That's what Mom calls it," Alex said with a chuckle.

"I don't feel like any time has passed. Talking to you right now feels just like it did then. We seem to have picked up right where we left off."

Alex nodded with a wistful smile. "It does."

Dana grinned. "Tell me about your love life."

Alex sipped her coffee and sighed. "I went through sort of a divorce a year ago. We weren't legally married, but we were together for ten years. For the last three, we drifted steadily apart, so the split wasn't a surprise to either of us, but it was still painful. I don't know when I'll be ready to date again."

Dana set her hand atop Alex's arm; the touch made her skin tingle. "I'm sorry."

Alex looked away. "Thanks. How about you?"

"I've been out in the dating world for a while, and it's brutal." Dana pulled her legs into the chair with her and wrapped her arms around them. "I get lonely—horny," she admitted with a laugh. She shrugged. "I don't know what's wrong with me. I haven't met anyone that grabs me, and I don't care." She sighed and looked up at the night sky. "The guys used to throw themselves at your feet. I'll bet when you're ready, there'll be a line of them outside your door."

Alex pursed her lips and met Dana's gaze. "I'm gay. When I do start looking, it won't be for a man."

Dana was stunned and felt her face heat when she turned and looked at Alex, unsure why. Her lips parted, but the power of speech failed her.

Alex's smile was tight. "Are we going to have a problem with that?"

"No...not at...all," Dana stammered. "You just surprised me. So...when did that happen?"

"I realized it when we were kids, I just never told you. It took me a while to come completely out of the closet."

Dana nodded as it all sank in. "That explains why you changed boyfriends like you did your socks. I used to think Evan Sicard was the hottest guy on the planet, and he followed you around like a puppy, but you were never interested." She chuckled. "Now I know why."

"He still lives here, and he's single, by the way. Wife number three left him a year ago when he tried to repair a hole in their roof with beer cans." Alex grinned. "I applauded him for recycling."

"Well, I'll keep that in mind. If I run out of troubles, I'll know where to find a new one," Dana said with a smile, then sobered. "Sometimes, I wonder if Sydney is gay. She has no interest in boys whatsoever. She had such a close relationship with a girl that I'd begun to think they were more than friends. When Leighton moved away, Sydney was seriously depressed, but she wouldn't talk to me about it. I just remind her that I'll listen to anything she has to say without judgment. That's kind of a lie. If she told me she was pregnant or robbing banks, I'd freak."

Alex met Dana's eye. "If she were a lesbian, how would you deal with it?"

"Well, we'd re-evaluate sleepovers, but I wouldn't treat her any differently otherwise. I know what a parent's disapproval of you does to your psyche. She's my daughter, and I love her more than myself. Nothing will change that."

Dana had changed, Alex noted as she gazed at her. She'd been a cute girl, but as a woman, she was truly pretty. Her features were delicate and soft, like a porcelain doll with its perfect high cheekbones, bright blue eyes, and small nose.

Alex smiled warmly. "You're a great mom."

"Yes, I am," Dana agreed with a nod. "But there are times that child makes me so mad I want to pull my hair out. When she gets it in her mind that she's going to do something, she's impossible to deal with."

"Whew," Alex said with a laugh. "That apple didn't fall far from the tree."

Dana pointed at Alex with a grin. "That's one of the things she does that reminds me of you. Shall I recount the story of when you decided that you were going to paint the water tower?"

Alex shrugged. "Hey, I learned my lesson, and I've never been arrested since. Wow, Dad was mad. I couldn't believe he let me spend the night in jail. Every time I fell asleep, one of the officers would bang on the bars and wake me up. When I got home the next day all bleary-eyed, Dad made me dig a ditch. I wasn't out there by myself for long. Both of my brothers joined me because he caught them laughing."

"Where are they? You didn't mention Andrew and Malcolm earlier."

Alex rolled her eyes. "Malcolm is a doctor, and he never fails to remind me of that. He's married with two kids, and they live in South Dakota, which is where his wife is from. Andy is actually gay, too. He and his partner live just outside of Atlanta."

"Where were you all the years that you were gone?"

Alex groaned when she spilled a drop of coffee on her shirt. She held up a hand. "I know you're going to say some things never change."

"Thank you for saving me the effort." Dana laughed. "Now answer the question."

Alex shrugged. "All over. I'm sure you recall that I just had to go to UCLA to study marine biology. I got all the way out there and decided that wasn't for me. I changed my major so many times I just ended up with a general studies degree, which was a waste of money. I met a woman, and we ended up in Utah. I met another woman, and we ended up in New York."

"I see a theme developing here. You basically travel with women like a gypsy."

Alex's smile was wry. "I did for a while. I got homesick and ended up back here for just a little while before I went to PA school in Shreveport. That's where I met Vanessa. She's an RN. I met her at the clinic I worked for up there. She has a sister who lives in Lafayette, so we ended up moving down here when I got a job with Dr. Morris. She commuted to the hospital in New Iberia, and we rented a house over on Aspen Lane."

"So you really wanted to come home."

Alex nodded. "Mom and Dad are getting older, and it's good to spend time with them. Someone is going to have to be around to take care of Maw Maw after they're gone because that woman is going to live forever."

Dana laughed. "I remember how she used to scowl at me."

"She still scowls."

"Does she still sing?"

Alex sank low in her chair. "Oh, dear God, yes. Every now and then, she'll get really tanked and turn nostalgic. She'll start belting out that old song, *Silver Wings*, but it sounds like silver wangs. When she sings something about them glowing in sunlight, it cracks me and Mom up, then she gets pissed at us for laughing. Maw Maw does *not* like to be the butt of a joke, but she sure can dish it." Alex looked at her watch and sat up straight. "I didn't realize it was so late. I should get home."

"I guess I need to go to bed." Dana stood and stretched. "I've got a job at Beaudreaux's Seafood, I'm the new logistics coordinator."

"Congratulations," Alex said with a bow. "If you ever feel the need to send a truckload of fresh shrimp my way, please don't hesitate."

Dana grinned and gave Alex a long lingering hug. "Thank you for coming to see me. I've missed you, and knowing you live here now is a huge comfort."

Alex pulled away and handed Dana her coffee cup. "I'm thrilled you're home, too. We'll get together sometime. I'd love to show you the house."

"Maybe we can do that this weekend?" Dana asked with a hopeful expression.

"Absolutely." Alex stepped off the porch. "Clara has my number. Give me a call on Friday."

"I will." Dana watched Alex go. It seemed so strange to watch her once again walk through patches of moonlight allowed in by the live oak tree. It reminded Dana that not all memories of home were bitter.

Chapter 6

"Hey, Ms. Alex," Sydney said brightly.

Alex gazed up from her menu and smiled. "Do not call me that, please. Alex is just fine. You look really cool in your apron."

"I feel like such a dork," Sydney said softly as she looked around. "But I'm happy because Mrs. Susan is letting me wait on one and two tops by myself, that's tables with only one or two people at them. Do you want tea mixed with lemonade?"

"Yes," Alex said with a nod. "Good memory. Half and half, please."

"Okay, I'll get that and be right back to get your order."

Alex watched her go and assumed that Sydney looked just like her father because the only part of Dana she recognized was a facial expression every now and then. She gazed back at the menu, which she knew by heart, as she thought about the visit with Dana the night before. She'd feared that seeing Dana again would open up old longings, but the only thing Alex had felt was the joy of reuniting with her dear friend. She wondered if perhaps with a little maturity it was easier for her heart to put things in their proper perspective.

Sydney returned and set the glass on the table along with a straw. "Have you decided what you'd like to have?"

"I want the chef salad with the house dressing and the meat on the side," Alex said as she handed the menu to Sydney.

"Okay, cornbread or French bread?"

"French, but only bring me one slice. If I have the basket, I'll eat the whole thing, and I don't want to do that. I get sleepy when I overeat, and you may find me in the fetal position under the table hugging a piece of bread." Alex grinned when Sydney laughed.

"I'll go put your order in. If you need anything, just wave and I'll be right back."

"Okay, thanks."

Alex thought about the kids she knew in town and who would be good to introduce Sydney to. She jumped when Sydney returned and said, "Okay, I'm back. Your order is in and you're my only table, so I thought I'd come over and see if I could hear some of those stories about Mom."

"Oh, you're gonna get me in trouble," Alex said with a laugh.

"A little one, and I won't tell her," Sydney pleaded with an impish grin.

Alex leaned up on the table. "One time, we decided to egg a guy's house because he stood your mom up. She'd just gotten her license, and she was driving your grandpa's car. She was too chicken to get out, so we did a drive-by, and she ended up hitting the top of the door with one of her eggs. It exploded all over her and the car, and what made it so bad was they were rotten."

"Oh, epic fail," Sydney said with a laugh. "One time when I was little, the woman in the apartment next to us got mad because I was riding my scooter on the sidewalk and she had to step off on the grass. So she just shoved me off of it. I was crying and all upset when I told Mom about it. She stomped outside, banged on the neighbor's door, and shoved her when she opened it. But it was the wrong neighbor, and the woman got all upset, so Mom baked her a cake. She did go after the woman that pushed me, and it wasn't pretty. The woman wouldn't open her door, so Mom broke one of her patio chairs." Sydney's big brown eyes widened. "I thought the woman was gonna call the cops because Mom's face was all red and her eyes were wild and she was saying stuff like, 'That's right, when I get my hands on you, I'm gonna tear your cushion off.'"

"Your mom was a scrapper. There was this girl that…" Alex shook a finger and laughed. "She'll have to tell you that story. Have you made any friends here yet?"

"I met a dude, he came in with his mom. I think his name was Bryce. He likes to skateboard, too, and we talked boards and stuff."

"Bryce Galloway, he has red hair?"

Sydney nodded. "Yep, that's him."

"He's a nice guy. I know him and his mom real well. Hey, are you off this weekend?"

"Sunday but not Saturday."

"I invited your mom to come out and see my place. Maybe we could grill up something on Sunday."

"And take your boat out?" Sydney asked with a gleam in her eyes. "Grandpa told me you have a ski boat."

Alex sat back and grinned. "You like to ski?"

Sydney nodded. "I can almost slalom. I learned with some friends last summer."

"Oh, we'll definitely have to get my dad to do a tune-up on it then, so we can hit the water. My folks have a pool at their place, so if you like to swim, we could go over there, too."

"Cool. I should go check on your food, be right back."

Alex made a mental note to get her father to service the boat. It was his, but after one summer, he lost interest in it. Wade would never admit how he came to be in possession of a ski boat since he preferred to fish, but Jean was certain that he'd traded the material for her gazebo that happened to be stolen while she was away with the girls for a weekend.

"Here's your salad with house dressing, meat on the side, and one slice of bread."

"You got it right. You don't know how often that doesn't happen." Sydney looked pleased with the praise, and Alex knew she'd go broke if she ate there every day because she was going to tip Sydney well.

"Bullshit, Danny. I know you stopped off at your girlfriend's house because I have eyes everywhere. If we get a late order, you're taking it. Now get those oysters to Houma before they spoil. You got me?" Lisa slammed the phone down and smiled at Dana, who was taking notes. "You may not want to follow my example on everything. Since I'm the boss's wife, I get away with a little more than most, but you've gotta be firm or they'll pull crap just like Danny tried to do by claiming he was stuck in traffic."

"Got it." Dana smiled, despite the turmoil she felt inside. She considered herself pretty good at multitasking, but she'd just watched Lisa talk on the phone and the radio at the same time, update information in the computer, and eat a bag of peanuts.

"You look scared, but don't be. This is like learning to ride a bike, you fall down a lot. Everything will click into place, I promise. You'll eat a lot in here, too. It just comes with the territory, and it eases the stress. That's why I bring peanuts and celery to munch on. Do you smoke?"

"No."

"You're gonna want to. That's not allowed in the building, but the last woman that worked in here puffed on one of those vapor thingies. She was like this really big dyke, and some of the guys were kind of scared of her because they weren't sure if they could beat her ass if they had to, so they didn't screw with her. You probably shouldn't get to know the drivers. Once they figure out you're nice, they're gonna try to run over you. Clint has a hard time keeping good drivers, so he babies them. You gotta be tough and firm, but not too hard on them that they whine."

Dana wondered if Lisa naturally talked incessantly or if she inhaled energy drinks on her breaks. She was worn out just listening to her. "How long did it take you to get a handle on all of this?"

Lisa looked up at the ceiling. "I felt like a monkey fucking a football for about two weeks, then it all started to make sense. But it was probably a month before I really got it all down. I'll be in here with you for that long, unless you feel like you've got it."

Dana sighed. "Good."

"I heard that you and Alex Soileau are good friends." Lisa clasped her hands together. "I just love her. I used to go to Dr. Morris every spring and summer with a bad sinus infection. He wasn't in one day, and Alex saw me. She said allergies were probably my problem, so I started taking an over-the-counter medicine, and I haven't been sick since. I know she's a lesbian, but she doesn't look like Blair did. Not to say that Blair wasn't nice-looking, she was just tough and kind of scared me. I have to tell you, that if I was going to jump the wire, I'd go for Alex. She's good-looking and smart and so, so sweet." She lowered her voice and scooted her chair close to Dana's. "I did have a one-night thing with a woman when Clint and I stayed at one of those resorts in Jamaica where everything goes. We went for hours. Sex with a woman is work! But, oh, the orgasms. She played my body like a fiddle. I kept hitting those high notes if you know what I mean. I'd do it again if the opportunity arose. Have you ever done that?"

Dana blinked for a second, fairly certain this conversation was inappropriate for the workplace, then realized she was supposed to say something. "Um…no, I've never been that adventurous, I suppose."

Lisa closed her eyes and bumped her forehead with her fist. "I always get in trouble for running my mouth too much. Did I offend you?"

"No, you didn't. It just takes me a minute or two to process what you're saying because you talk so fast."

Lisa grinned sheepishly. "I've done that all my life. My momma used to look at me and say, 'Lisa, I love you, honey, but if you don't shut up for five seconds, you're gonna find me jumping off a bridge somewhere.' So I'd just go outside and talk to the dog, but after a while, he wouldn't even listen to me. I'd walk out on the porch, and he'd take off running like I'd beaten him. Of course, that's probably why I'm also on my third marriage, and I'm not even thirty. Clint has a hearing problem because he worked as an engineer on the boats and the motors were loud, so he has to wear a little tiny hearing aid that you can barely see. He looks at me and smiles when I talk, but I'm sure he shuts that thing off when he wants to. I think he can read lips, though, because if I mention the words money or shopping, he perks right up and goes to fussing."

Mercifully, the phone rang, and Lisa answered it. Dana rubbed her temples, resigned to the fact that she was going to have to learn by watching. The only knowledge she'd gained thus far was that some lubricants made Lisa's lips swell—the ones on her face, she was quick to point out. Also, which drivers had tight asses, Lisa liked to do squats to keep her ass from getting numb in the chair, her bra began to feel too tight after three in the afternoon, she had a fling with a woman, and Clint wore a hearing aid.

Sydney climbed out of the car and stretched her back. She thought the shoes that the other waitresses wore were hideous with their big thick soles, but she was beginning to see the logic after being on her feet all day. Free food, especially pie, and tips soothed her discomfort. She was about to go into the house when she noticed her grandpa sitting out in his chair and decided to discuss paying for her truck. Change and bills filled the pockets of her jeans, and she felt rich as she walked over to him.

"Hey, Grandpa."

Daniel looked up at her and smiled. "Join me." He gestured to the other chair and set his book aside. "How are things at the diner?"

"Great." Sydney plopped down and grinned. "I made forty dollars in tips today, and I didn't even work the dinner shift. Mrs. Susan says I'm doing a good job, and in a few days, I'll be able to wait the larger tables without a trainer."

Daniel's brow rose. "If you could average forty dollars a day for a week, you'd have two hundred bucks in tips alone."

"Yes, sir, I think I'm gonna be making some bank, so I need to talk to you about a truck note. How much do you want to charge me?"

"Sydney," he began gently, "the truck is a gift. I enjoyed driving it, but the issues that affect a person my age make that impossible now. It would make me happy to know that you're enjoying it just as much. I understand how your mother feels, so in respect, you may pay me twenty-five cents a week. I bought her first car, so I feel I should be able to do the same for you."

"Grandpa, that's not fair."

"That's my offer, take it or leave it."

"I'll take it," Sydney said with a squeal as she jumped up and hugged him.

Daniel chuckled and patted her on the back. "How're the driving lessons going?"

"Okay." Sydney sat back down with a sigh. "I know I can get it, I just have to practice. Mom can't dribble a ball and walk at the same time, so if she can drive a stick, I know I'll be able to do it."

"Do you and your mother get along well?" Daniel asked as he gazed at her.

"Most of the time. I mean, we're better than some of my friends and their moms. Dedee, she's a friend back home, her mother is a total B. Like when Dedee has a bad day and she's all upset, her mother says, 'So what do you want me to do about it?' All Dedee wants is a hug. Her mom fusses at her about not spending time with the family when she wants to hang with her friends, but when she's at home, her mother stays in the bedroom with her boyfriend. Mom's in my grill a lot, but she listens when I have a bad day, and I get hugs…sometimes too many, which is kind of irritating. She doesn't bring all kinds of men home, either. A lot of my friends have to deal with that. So she's cool, but she's still a mom if you know what I mean."

"What…is your grill?"

"Oh," Sydney said with laugh. "That means in my face. Retract the claws means calm down, and adorkable means adorable but dorky."

Daniel nodded as he studied her face. "What does your mother like to do?"

Sydney shrugged. "She reads and watches movies. She works…or worked a lot when we were home. She really didn't have a lot of time to go places. We had a little garden on our patio at the apartment, and she really liked to plant things. I guess if she had a hobby, that was it."

"She must get that from my mother." Daniel pointed to a patch of lawn near the marsh. "If you can imagine it, she had a beautiful garden out there surrounded by a white picket fence. Inside, she grew flowers and vegetables, and at times, strawberries. There were days I hid in it and ate all the berries I could."

"What happened to it?"

"My wife, your grandmother, had what they call a 'black thumb,' she couldn't grow a thing. One day, I bought her a plant in a pot, and it was dead a week later. The untended garden became an eyesore, so I had the fence removed and the weeds inside cut down." Daniel sighed as he stared at the plot of land. "Nature has a subtle way of teaching us lessons. Beautiful things grow under a loving hand, but when neglected, they become…" He cleared his throat as his gaze returned to Sydney. "Your mother has done a fine job tending you. I don't know anything about plants, but I would say that you are a beautiful flower that continues to bloom just like your mother."

Chapter 7

Alex had just peeled a banana and was about to take a bite Friday evening when her phone rang. It broke off and fell at her feet just as she said, "Hello?"

"Hi, Alex, it's Dana."

"Hey, girl, how's the new job?"

There was a moment of silence, then Dana replied, "Good...it's interesting."

"Sydney waited on me the other day, did she tell you?"

"Yes," Dana said with a tone. "She also told me you tipped her twenty bucks for a salad."

"I'm very particular about my food. I like meat, I like salad, but I don't like them together in the same bowl, it's a thing. Sydney got my order right on the first try. I felt like that should be rewarded. We talked about this weekend, and I understand that she's off Sunday. I thought a cookout might be fun, are you interested?"

"Absolutely, what can I bring?"

"Your swimsuits. I don't know if the boat will be ready by then, but there's the pool at Mom and Dad's."

"Alex, it's May, the water's still cold."

"Still a pansy."

"I am *not* a pansy. Just because I refused to jump off the roof of your house onto the trampoline doesn't make me a wimp, it makes me sensible. That broken arm still give you trouble?"

"I was a baby, my bones were rubbery, and it's just fine, thank you. Would you like to come over around noon?"

"That sounds perfect, but aside from swimwear, what can I bring?"

Alex bit her bottom lip. "You wouldn't happen to know how to make your mother's potato salad?"

"Yes, I do. I also know how to make her Mississippi mud pie."

Alex squeezed the peel in her hand, and the rest of the banana shot out on the floor. "Oh…yes! Bring that, too. I'll take care of everything else. Do you still remember how to get here?"

"I do, and I'll bring a pocket full of change," Dana said with a laugh.

"Great! I'll see you then."

"Okay, call me if you think of anything else I should bring. I'm really looking forward to this."

"Me too," Alex said with a smile. "See you soon."

When the call ended, Alex looked at the piece of banana near her foot. It was covered in sheetrock dust, as was the living room. The floor was covered with plastic sheeting from when she and her father textured the living room walls. She was currently using two buckets of plaster and a board as her coffee table. Her couch and the rest of her furniture was shrink-wrapped. She inhaled sharply. "Time to paint and clean."

After a change of clothes and a protein shake, she turned on some music and got to work. The windows were open, and the afternoon breeze blew softly through the house. Alex hummed along with an eighties tune as she poured the paint into a tray. Springtime always made her nostalgic and reminded her of a time in her life so long ago. It seemed like a dream.

Dana looked over her shoulder. "He's following us."

"I know," Alex said as she stared straight ahead.

"He's so cute. Why don't you like him?"

"He smells funny, and he gets on my nerves. Cute doesn't always mean cool."

Dana sighed. "You're so lucky. I can't wait to be seventeen and date. I hope I have boys chasing after me then."

Alex rolled her eyes. "Boys like you now."

"Yeah, but Daddy won't let me date any. He used to say I had to be sixteen and now it's seventeen. I heard him tell Momma that he's going to make me wait until I'm seventeen to get my driver's license. But she said that was too close to me being eighteen and I'd be going off to school without a lot of driving experience. She thinks I should get my license as soon as possible, so they can teach me." Dana kicked at a rock, churning up dust on the gravel road.

"Trust me when I say you ain't missing anything when it comes to dating. When you get to the trail that leads to the blackberry patches, run down it. We're gonna lose old smelly."

Dana giggled. "Okay."

"Go."

Dana took off running like a small rabbit, and Alex followed close on her heels. They ran past the thorny patches to an area where young trees had been choked out by vines and formed a green maze. Alex grabbed Dana by the shirt and pulled her against one of the vined walls and put a finger to her lips. They listened as Evan Sicard thudded along the trail griping all the way.

"Mean bitches. Stupid stickers. Alex, wait up!"

When he passed close to where they hid, Dana backed up a step and leaned into Alex. For a split second, Alex liked the closeness, then in the next second, she was repulsed. Dana was a baby, someone to be looked after. Alex moved away, feeling like a depraved pervert. The sound drew Evan's attention, and when Alex tried to sneak out of the maze, they came face to face. It was a gut reaction, and she sent Evan hurtling into the vines.

"You bitch," he howled as he tried to disentangle himself, making his predicament worse. Alex took off running again with Dana behind her, and she heard Evan call after her, "I love you."

"Aw," Dana said when they'd put some distance between them and Evan. "He loves you."

"Dana, that's what boys say when they don't really know you but want to have sex with you. He's lucky I didn't go back and punch him in the mouth."

Alex smiled as she ran the paint roller over the wall. She did punch Evan in the mouth once and laid him out after he groped her in the checkout line at the grocery store. He hadn't spoken to her since, and she was just fine with that.

The next morning, Dana's eyes flew open wide, and she stared at the ceiling of her bedroom, trying to figure out the grating noise she was hearing. She looked at the clock and frowned. It was just after six, and whoever was responsible was in grave danger. She threw her covers aside and got up. The noise was louder in the hallway when she stepped into Sydney's room. The French doors were open, and she could see Sydney standing on the veranda.

"What're they doing?" Dana asked as she joined her and noticed one man running a tiller, while two more bore deep holes in the ground with an auger.

"I think...it's my fault," Sydney said.

Dana ran a hand through her hair and yawned. "Why?"

"Because Grandpa asked me what you liked to do, and I told him it was gardening. He told me that his mom used to have one where those guys are working." Sydney turned to Dana. "I think he's making you one." Sydney kissed her on the cheek. "I have to go, or I'm gonna be late for work."

Stupefied, Dana mumbled, "Have a good day, baby."

She remembered seeing old black-and-white photos of her grandmother's garden surrounded by a wooden fence. The gate had an archway over it covered in flowering vines; hydrangeas grew on either side of it. Dana couldn't help but be touched as she put a hand to her chest.

She went back inside, brushed her teeth, and got dressed

in a pair of shorts and a tank top. Downstairs, she found Clara alone in the kitchen. "What's going on outside?"

"I asked the same question this morning when the men showed up, but your father wouldn't say." Clara didn't meet Dana's gaze and turned her back to her as she washed some fruit. "I think it's going to be a garden."

Dana narrowed her eyes. "Do you garden?"

"Oh, Lord, no. I'll cook up a storm, but Clara Ford does not put her hands in the earth."

"Does Dad garden?"

Clara released a little laugh. "He can barely bend down to tie his shoes. Most mornings, I have to do it for him."

"Then who is the garden for?"

Clara shook her head. "I have no idea, none at all."

"Is Dad senile?"

"Forgetful, but he still has all his mental faculties. Rather sharp, I'd say."

Dana put a hand on her hip. "Would you turn around and look at me?"

Clara stopped what she was doing and hesitated for a second before she turned. "Yes?" she asked with an impish grin as she looked everywhere but at Dana.

"I know now that I can never tell you a secret. You're horrible at being evasive."

Clara released a little giggle as she clenched her fists. "Well, there's no sense in trying to hide it, it's out in the open. Your father was like a little boy last night. I don't know if I've ever seen him so excited. He had me call Nate Spearman, his son has a lawn business, that's who tends this one. Anyway, Daniel got on the phone with them and told them to be out here first thing regardless of the cost. He wanted the land tilled and a fence built around it. He's off with Nate right now shopping for gardening tools. He was a man on a mission this morning, even dressed in a pair of those safari-looking shorts and a straw hat."

Clara took in a deep breath and seemed to get a hold of herself as she took Dana's hand.

"I don't know the full extent of what happened between the two of you. I think he'd be very upset with me for telling you this, so please don't mention it. When you called and said you needed to come home, he hung up the phone and began making a list of things he wanted done. There's a cleaning service that comes here once a week, but he had them come out and clean up this place top to bottom, same thing with the yard. Neither was in bad shape, but he wanted it just right. He had me shop for every kind of food and drink imaginable." Clara smiled as she squeezed Dana's hand. "I heard him tell one of the workmen when he asked the reason for the extra spiffing that 'my baby is coming home.' He can be abrupt and distant at times, there have been occasions that he has really hurt my feelings, so I can only imagine what you dealt with. But he's doing his best to make you happy here. I think he feels a sense of purpose that he hasn't felt in a long time, and whether he shows it or not, he is thrilled to have you home."

Dana felt light-headed as she pulled away from Clara and went to the table where she sat down.

"Oh, I've upset you," Clara said fretfully. She hurriedly filled a cup with coffee and brought it to the table.

"I wonder sometimes if he confuses me with Mary," Dana said as she stared at the cup Clara set in front of her.

Clara took a seat. "Why would you think that?"

"The other day, he told Sydney that I had a duck and I used to catch turtles when I was little, but that was Mary."

"I have two sons, and I often confuse memories of their antics back then. I still blame James for dropping a frog into the washer when it was on spin when it was actually Carter. That poor frog hopped sideways when I pulled it out of the wash, but he smelled nice."

Dana propped her chin in her hand. "Everything changed when Mary died. We used to do things as a family, but that stopped. Dad would come home from work, go into his office, and close the door. He wouldn't even look at me for the longest time. When he finally did...he just seemed so cold, and everything out of his mouth was a rule or condemnation for the things I did wrong. If it hadn't been for Mom, I would've run away. When I turned eighteen, I basically did."

"I think he's trying to tell you in his way that he loves you," Clara said gently.

"It would've been cheaper than hiring a lawn crew if he'd just said, 'Hey, I love you.' That would've had an impact, too."

"Sometimes, he's a difficult man to understand."

"You got that right," Dana said with a sigh.

They quieted when the back door opened and Daniel walked in with a bag banging against his cane. His gaze fell on Dana as he said, "You're up early this morning."

She tried to act casual. "There was a lot of noise outside."

"Yes." Daniel shuffled over to the table and laid the bag next to Dana. "Sydney told me that you like to garden. The men outside are making you one. They'll be finished by the end of the weekend. I bought you some accoutrements, and there are more outside. There's also a certificate inside that will allow you to pick out what you'd like to plant." Daniel turned and walked toward the den.

Dana got up and followed him. From behind, she wrapped her arms around his waist and hugged him. "Thank you, Dad, that was very kind."

Daniel didn't turn when she released him. "You're welcome," he said as he continued to shuffle on.

Dana quietly crept into her father's study with her fingers crossed that the box of old family photos would still be in the bottom drawer of the armoire. It slid open easily, and the polished wooden box still rested in the corner. Carefully, she lifted it out, went to the door, listened for a moment, and ran up the stairs. In the improvised den, she set the box on the coffee table and breathed in the scent of old photo paper as she opened it.

On top of the stack was a photo taken of the family when she was nine. Daniel and Audrey sat side by side with big smiles for the camera. Dana and Mary knelt in front of them. They were happy then, it was obvious. Dana set the photo aside with the idea of framing it, then changed her mind. Being in her childhood home was enough to remind her of what used to be. She dug a little deeper and pulled out another.

The image made her smile. "Oh, Alex, someone should've told you not to wear those tube socks. Someone should've told me not to tease my hair that high."

She and Alex stood side by side. Alex had one arm draped over Dana's shoulders. Alex's hair was long then, at least to the middle of her back. As Dana stared at her face, it struck her that at that age Alex and Sydney favored. As Dana sat back and studied it, she was reminded of the night she met Sydney's father.

He'd reminded her of Alex the minute they met. Lonesome for someone familiar, Dana was drawn to him, but the man she married was not the best friend she'd sought. As Dana looked back on it, she knew as she stood in front of the justice of the peace speaking her vows that she wasn't in love with Troy Elliot. She craved stability and companionship and thought marriage would provide her with that. She'd been too impulsive and realized that she'd made a huge mistake almost the second the ring was placed on her finger. What the marriage lacked, Sydney provided when she arrived. When Troy left her, it was a relief.

Dana set the picture of her and Alex aside and continued to dig until she found what she was looking for. She had remembered correctly—hydrangeas were planted on either side of the gate. Clematis vines covered the arch. She couldn't tell what grew inside, but she did see beans growing over the sides of the fence. To show her appreciation for Daniel's gift, Dana was determined to make the new garden look like the original.

After the picture box was returned to its place, Dana wandered back upstairs with the two photos in her hand. The late afternoon breeze was cool as it blew across the balcony overlooking the front yard. She tapped the photos in her hand on the railing as memories flooded her mind.

Dana's hands burned as she jogged down her street, hiding behind shrubs every so often when a car passed. She'd slipped coming down the live oak and skinned her palms, but she considered the pain worth it to be able to see Alex in her prom dress. Since Alex had refused to model it, Dana was forced to sneak to the school and peek in on the dance.

Cars moved in and out of the school parking lot as Dana sneaked around to the back gym entrance that she knew would be open since there was no air-conditioning. She could hear music and laughing as she drew close and pressed her body to the wall next to the door. Slowly, she looked around the frame and scanned the people inside as a disco ball twirled overhead.

Keith Gauthier was doing his best Michael Jackson in the middle of the dance floor, even though a Billy Idol song played over the sound system. A few guys slam danced. And then Mark Lanoux, Alex's date, crossed Dana's line of sight. She watched as he wove his way through the crowd.

"Oh, she would have to hang out in the one place I can't see her," Dana grumbled aloud.

The bleachers had been folded up, and Dana knew there was a gap between them and the wall. If she was fast enough, she could get behind them without being detected, then she could travel to the other side of the gym. Dana took a good look around for any chaperones who might spot her and took off when the coast was clear. Behind the bleachers, she stepped over pencils and paper airplanes and avoided wads of gum. She'd lucked out at the other end because the photo backdrop had been set up there, and it made a great place to hide. But the second she peeked around it, she caught the eye of Aimee Perkins, class bitch.

Aimee stuck her head behind the backdrop. "What're you doing here, dweeb?"

Dana stared up at the mass of white blond hair swept back

and sprayed into a giant bouffant. "I'm dropping off something, George Washington, so mind your own business and piss off."

The second Aimee stormed away, Dana looked for a new place to hide because she knew she was going to be ratted out. She dropped to her knees and crawled through the stickiness of spilled soda and punch, then slipped under one of the snack tables. An opening where two tablecloths met allowed her to spy on the promgoers. She could hear Alex's voice and knew she was close, but someone in a royal blue satiny dress with cascading layers blocked her view. She sank lower and tried to look through the girl's knees where the dress stopped.

"Come on, dance with me, Alex. You said you would on a slow song."

"Fine" followed a dramatic sigh. "Just one and I don't wanna go far. I can barely walk in these shoes."

Dana was so happy to see the blue dress move away from the table, then she realized that Alex was actually in it. She gawked open-mouthed at the off-the-shoulder outfit with a tight bodice that revealed Alex had cleavage—very small, but it was there. Normally, she wore her hair in a ponytail or parted it on the side and just let it hang, but that evening, it was swept up on one side, and her bangs were teased impossibly high. Alex had on makeup, too; her eyelids glittered all the way up to her brows. She wasn't the Alex that Dana knew, but she still thought with a smile that Alex was the prettiest girl there.

Mark leaned in and tried to kiss her. Alex turned her face away. "I got gum," she said as she smacked it.

Dana's brow furrowed as her smile faded. She felt a weird tug in the pit of her stomach as she watched Alex in Mark's arms, a strange feeling of sadness swept through her. Dana wondered if it was envy because where Alex was she wanted to be there, too, and she wasn't allowed this time. Or maybe it was because she knew Alex didn't want to be there. She'd said it a million times, but her mom insisted she go. Whatever it was settled deep inside of Dana and stayed with her even when she sneaked back home.

Chapter 8

"You can't cook in here. Half the kitchen still isn't unpacked." Jean shook her head as she looked around. "Alexandra, you've been living in this house for eight months."

"And it's been under construction the whole time," Alex said with a grunt as she and her father moved the sofa into place. "My bedroom's set up, go look in there."

"You're not going to be preparing a meal in there." Jean picked up a package of paper plates. "Are these what you've been eating off of?"

"You act like I've been eating cereal out of my shoe," Alex blustered.

Jean tossed the paper plates aside. "Where are your dishes?"

"Probably still in the Sea-Can behind your house. It makes no sense to unpack everything if I'm just going to gut the kitchen anyway."

Jean put a hand on her hip. "You can't seriously be considering entertaining company with this house still in the shape it's in."

"I certainly am," Alex said, mimicking her mother's pose. "It's not the pope, it's Dana and her daughter, Sydney."

"All the more reason to move this party to our house. You're already coming over to swim. You should eat there, as well. I want to see Dana and meet her daughter."

Alex nodded. "You will when we swim."

Jean turned to her husband. "Wade, back me up."

He threw up his hands. "Listen to your mother."

"I am, I just don't like what I'm hearing. What's wrong with my house?"

Wade shrugged. "Nothing."

"Wade!" Jean barked.

"Alex, listen to your mother."

"I painted all night Friday, and I spent yesterday installing the molding and cleaning the floors in here, so it would be presentable."

"But the kitchen isn't, and you're cooking," Jean argued.

"Grilling, we'll be on the porch."

Jean clasped her hands together and gritted her teeth. "Alexandra, if you value her friendship, do not make her eat in this abomination of a kitchen."

Alex threw up her hands. "Fine, I'll go to your house and steal the fine china, will that make you happy?"

"No! Bring Dana and Sydney to our house to eat with us, that will make me...us...happy. Right, Wade?"

Wade nodded, and when he glanced at Alex, he shook his head to the contrary. "Isn't there more furniture we have to move?"

Jean glared at him. "Honey, do you want to be sleeping here tonight?"

"Alex, listen to your mother," Wade said as he walked outside.

Jean squared her shoulders. "All right, it's just you and me, girl. You can lie and play nonchalant, but I know you had a crush on Dana when you were—"

"All right! We cook and eat at your place. I'll show Dana and Sydney the house because Dana *wants* to see it, then we'll come over."

"Why won't you talk to me about her?" Jean followed Alex into her bedroom. "Oh, wow, it is nice in here. Good job, baby." Jean walked over to where Alex was digging in her dresser. "Why is that subject taboo?"

"She's straight, and that was a long time ago. There's nothing more to discuss." Alex pulled out a pair of shorts. "Do these match the shirt I'm wearing?"

"No." Jean shook her head. "I'm shocked you had to ask. You are your father's child. Wear something nice."

"I'm fresh out of cocktail dresses, and I'm going to be next to a hot grill in the sun because at your place it's out in the open. I'm totally going for comfort." Alex pulled out a white tank top sporting a stain or two.

Jean snatched it out of her hand and shook it. "You should be dusting with this, not wearing it. What about that white sleeveless button-down?"

Alex scowled. "That's a work shirt."

"Wear the black tank top with the pair of burgundy running shorts you have. It makes you look…svelte, and no one will notice if you get sauce all over yourself."

One of Alex's brows shot up. "Good point. I'll roll with it. Now step out, I need to change."

"Honey, I've seen everything you've got. I changed your diapers."

"What I've got is grown, and you don't need to see it now."

"Brush your hair." Jean started to walk out and turned. "Oh, and wear that lotion I like, the one that smells so clean."

Alex batted her eyes. "Maybe when I'm done, you can paint my toenails."

"Really?"

"No. Out."

"What time will you come to the house?" Jean asked excitedly.

"Sometime after noon. Dana's bringing potato salad and dessert. I have ribs and chicken."

"Okay, I'll just throw a few things together, nothing elaborate," Jean said with a wave as she walked out.

"Oh, boy," Alex said with a sigh. "The spread is on." She pulled the tank top and shorts Jean mentioned from another drawer and stared at them. "Svelte...obviously Jean's way of saying I look bloated."

Dana stared out the window as Sydney hopped them along in her new truck. "This road brings back so many memories. A lot of the houses you see weren't here when I was growing up. It was mostly woods. There was an old man with a wishing well...that's what we called it," Dana said with a laugh. "For some reason, he bricked a circle around a hole in the ground. All the kids were drawn to it like a magnet. We'd all sneak out here and make our wishes."

"Did any come true?" Sydney asked.

Dana smiled as she turned to her. "One sure did. I got you."

Sydney grinned. "You're so adorkable."

"Oh, I meant to tell you, Alex is a lesbian, so don't stare at her all stupefied like I did if she mentions it."

Sydney glanced at Dana. "Way to go, Mom, so not cool."

"It wasn't that I didn't approve or thought any different of her, I just didn't expect that to come flying out of her mouth."

"How could you not know? I totally got that vibe the minute I met her."

Dana's brow shot up. "You got a vibe?"

"Yeah, she's not butch, but she doesn't look like a soccer mom, either." Sydney shrugged. "I don't know what it is, I just knew. I like her, she's cool."

"I love her to death, she's a great friend. I shouldn't have let so much time pass...wait, do I look like a soccer mom?"

Sydney smirked and stared straight ahead.

"I've always gotten the impression people mean frumpy when they say soccer mom. Seriously, is that me?"

"I did play soccer for a couple of seasons, so technically, that does make you a soccer mom."

Dana looked down at her cutoff shorts and white cami top. "But do I look like one?"

"No, you look cool. When you wear those velour-looking yoga pants, that's so soccer mom."

Dana folded her arms. "Should I dress like Tonya Bell's mom?"

"No, that's hoochie. Walking around with a thong hanging out of the top of your pants and a shirt that shows off the muffin top isn't cool for anyone. But on the other end of the stick are the women who wear the peasant-style shirts and knee shorts."

"I don't wear any of those things," Dana retorted.

"I know, and I'm so glad. Just stay away from the velour and don't cut your hair off again."

Dana threw her hands up. "What was wrong with my hair?"

Sydney laughed. "You looked like someone stuck a cantaloupe over your head and cut out a square for your face."

Dana gasped. "You little fart. Slow way down because I'm not sure which driveway goes up to the house." Dana sat up on the edge of her seat. "I think it's this one."

Sydney shifted into neutral and sort of coasted onto the gravel lane. Dana struggled to hold on to the bowl of potato salad in her lap. "Hey, don't look at me like that, I'm still learning." Sydney shifted into second gear, and the truck lugged.

Dana smiled. "I have no complaints. You're doing a good job."

"She sure lives up in the woods. I don't know if I could do that by myself." Sydney shuddered. "It's swampy-looking."

"We used to tramp through all of that in shorts and sneakers," Dana said with a laugh.

Sydney gave her a sideways glance. "You were brave back then."

"No, just stupid."

As they came into the clearing near the house, the first thing Dana noticed was the wishing well. It was no longer surrounded by brush. Alex had even built an old-fashioned cover over it. A little bucket filled with flowers hung from a rope. It reminded her of wells she'd seen in storybooks. Dana wasn't sure she ever knew what the house looked like. They never got too close to it as children because it was surrounded by overgrowth, and Mr. Wicker wasn't the friendly sort.

She climbed out of the truck as she gazed up at the house on stilts with its high-pitched roof and wraparound deck. "I had no idea this place was this big when I was a kid. There wasn't even a yard, it was all trees, brush, and vines."

Alex walked onto the deck and smiled. "You found me."

"I did, but I got a little nervous on the road for a few seconds because I couldn't remember which driveway it was."

"I've got good news and bad," Alex said as she came down the stairs. "Mom came over this morning and decided that my house was unacceptable for entertaining, so she wants us to go to her place."

"I'd love to see her, that's not bad news," Dana said with a smile.

Alex's next comment was more directed at Sydney when she said, "The boat has some issues, but Dad's working on it. I don't think we'll be able to take it out today, but we will soon."

Sydney shrugged. "That's okay."

"The pool is good, though, so we can swim. Did you bring your suits?"

"We did," Dana said with a nod. "We'll just leave the food in the truck and you can ride with us over there, but I want to see the house first."

"Come on up." Alex went ahead of them on the stairs. "I still have a lot of work to do on it, so judge me kindly." She opened one of the French doors and held it for Dana and Sydney.

They stepped into the living room, and the first thing Dana noticed was the high ceilings that gave the area an open and airy feel. "Is that a loft up there?"

"It is," Alex said with a nod.

"Cool, can I go look at it?" Sydney asked.

Alex pointed to the stairs that ran up the wall over the hallway entrance. "Be my guest." She turned and smiled at Dana. "Let me show you the disaster area that is the kitchen. All you have to do is turn around."

It adjoined the living room and had plenty of windows overlooking the bay. The laminate countertops were cracked and stained; several cabinet doors were missing altogether. Alex had made a little table out of a piece of wood and two sawhorses. On top of it was a loaf of bread, a few canned goods, a box of finishing nails, and a pry bar. The appliances had all been removed except for a refrigerator that looked relatively new.

"I was going to cook outside, then we'd eat in the den, but Mom found this idea extremely offensive," Alex said.

Dana shrugged. "I wouldn't have minded at all. This room has great potential, and the views are gorgeous."

Sydney sounded like a little buffalo coming down the stairs. "The loft is totally cool. If this house was mine, I'd put my bedroom up there."

"I thought about that, but there's no door, it's just wide open. If I have company, I'll have no privacy, so I was thinking about using it as an office. My room is cool, though, come see." Alex led them through the living room and into the hallway. "First, the guest bath."

"Whoa!" Dana said with a laugh when Alex flipped on the lights. "Check out the pineapple express. Tell me you didn't do this."

"No," Alex said with a grin, "but you have to admit the pineapple-shaped faucets are kind of awesome."

Dana shook her head as she stepped in. "Not even a little bit." She stood in awe of the white wallpaper covered in metallic gold pineapples and the yellow sinks, toilet, and bathtub.

"Mom, you're being a little insulting," Sydney said.

"No, she's not," Alex said with a smile. "She knows I find this room absolutely hideous. They decorated the master bath the exact same way, must've gotten bargain prices on the pineapples. The first thing I did was gut it."

Dana and Sydney followed her down the hall. "Wow! Now this makes all renovations worthwhile," Dana said as she admired the view of the bay. "I love the high ceilings in here and the natural wood beams." She gazed at Alex's bed. "Your headboard even matches the wood above, and I think the stark white of the walls makes a terrific contrast." She ran her hand over the wide-striped navy blue and white comforter. "I think it's awesome."

Alex held up a finger and flipped the switch in her bathroom. Dana laughed and shook her head. "A tub with a view."

"I close the blinds when I get in and out, but when I'm lying in there, sometimes I open them and watch the sunset."

Dana gazed at the glass-walled corner shower and the contemporary glass sink bowls. I'm so impressed."

"Thanks," Alex said with a smile. "I'm pretty proud of it, especially since Dad and I did just about all the work. I went way over budget in here because I got carried away. That's why it's taking me a little while to finish the rest." She led them through the other two bedrooms, which were empty but at least painted and the floors were refinished. "The pineapple bathroom and the kitchen are all I have left to do, and both of those will be big jobs."

Alex dropped a hand on Sydney's shoulder as they walked back into the living room. "Let me tell you about Maw Maw. One thing you never do is ask how she's doing, or you'll spend hours listening to her tell you how she's dying. She's mean and likes to run over your feet with her electric scooter. She's drunk most of the time and will say the most outlandish things, so just ignore her. Try not to make eye contact. My mother will yell at her, so don't let that rattle you."

"Okay," Sydney said slowly.

"I see she hasn't changed a bit, except she has wheels now," Dana said with a laugh. "Hey, can I have a closer look at the well before we go?"

"Yes," Alex said with a smile. "I may even allow you to make a wish."

Dana followed Alex outside with Sydney on her heels. "I love the cover you built over it. The little clapboard shingles are a nice touch. Have you ever drained it to see how much money was in the bottom?" Dana asked.

Alex grinned at her. "You're gonna get a kick out of this story. Do you remember how it always stunk?"

"Yes," Dana said with reservation.

"Well, it turns out that the place where we made our wishes was a homemade septic tank, which explains why they never came true. We were tossing our money right into the crapper."

Sydney laughed. "Way to go, Mom. I feel so special."

Dana looked at Alex. "I told her on the way over here that I wished for her in the well. Now we all know why I got a little turd."

Sydney gave Dana a playful shove.

"It's not a sewer now," Alex explained. "I had it pumped out, then drilled. It's full of bay water."

Sydney walked up to it and looked over the circular wall. "So it's kind of a real well now."

"Not really, the water is brackish." Alex made a face. "I'd never use it even if it was fresh."

Dana reached into her pocket and pulled out some coins. "My wishes might finally come true now."

Sydney emptied her pockets and was about to toss a whole handful of change into the well. "New skateboard, camera, a gas tank that never goes empty, million bucks—"

Dana held up a finger. "Okay, you can't just throw, there's a method. One at a time, you drop your coin in, close your eyes, visualize the wish, and make it."

"And you don't tell what it is," Alex added, "unless you don't want it to come true. You go first, Sydney."

"Y'all are so goofy." Sydney stepped up to the well and dropped in her change despite Dana's instruction. She closed her eyes for a second and held up a thumb. "I'm done."

Alex gave Dana a nudge. She dropped her coin in and closed her eyes, but oddly couldn't think of what she wanted to wish for. It seemed wrong to her to waste a wish on a need. She'd always believed that wishes were made for the heart. *I wish for that perfect someone who will love me wholeheartedly and I love the same way. Someone special who will cherish my daughter. With a great sense of humor, great smile, who can cook...great in bed—*"

"Mom, sheesh."

Dana opened her eyes. "All right, I'm done, Ms. Impatient." She handed Alex a coin. "Your wish is on me."

"Thank you." Without preamble, Alex tossed the coin in. Her eyes were only closed a second, then she too said, "Done."

"That was a quick wish," Dana said with a laugh.

Alex put a hand on her hip. "I wished that Maw Maw would behave herself, and we all know that isn't gonna happen, so I don't fear telling it."

They loaded into the truck and drove a mile down the road. Jean's house smelled of baked beans, and the center island in the kitchen was full of dishes. Alex rolled her eyes as she took it all in. Her casual barbecue had been turned into a full-on feast.

"Oh, my God!" Jean wailed as she threw her arms around Dana's neck. "It's been ages. I feel like we're going back in time having you here. I was just reminiscing this morning about how you and Alex used to wreck the kitchen making cookies. Oh, I miss those days. I've missed you."

"I've missed you, too," Dana said as she reveled in the embrace. "You were like my second momma."

Jean pulled back and patted Dana's cheek. "I still am, little girl." She noticed Sydney standing next to Alex and gasped. "You've grown into a beautiful young woman. The last time I saw you, you were just a tiny little thing!" Sydney was treated to a hug, as well, then Jean stared at her for a moment. "You really remind me of Alex when she was your age. Y'all kind of favor."

Alex grinned at Sydney. "That means you're a good-looking kid."

Jean swatted at her. "Arrogant ass, go warm the grill and let me get reacquainted with Dana. Did you soak the ribs?"

"All night, Mother." Alex looked at Sydney. "The grill is on the pool deck, wanna come with me?"

"Sure." Sydney gave her mother a catty look. "The good-looking ones are going outside."

"My mother likes to fawn, so don't be surprised if she gets into your hair and pats your cheek a lot. If it starts to bother you, just give me a look and I'll call her off," Alex said as they walked across the lawn.

"I'm used to it. Mom's the same way." Sydney stepped inside the pool gate when Alex opened it for her and inhaled sharply. "Alex...I think your maw maw is dead," she said shakily.

Bobbing on the surface of the water on her back was Thelma. A pack of cigarettes had floated out of her shirt pocket. Her wiglet had become detached and was drifting toward one of the pump intakes like a black mass of seaweed.

"She's not dead," Alex said with a sigh. "I've never seen anyone whose entire body was that buoyant. I think it's the flubber. Dad wants to send her out in the bay and see if we can catch crabs off of her." Alex walked over to the edge of the pool and squatted down and splashed Thelma. "Hey, your hairpiece is headed into the skimmer baskets again."

Thelma's eyes flew open. "Shiat! Go get it, that's the last black one I have."

Alex stood and shook her head. "You got in with your cigarettes in your pocket again." She pulled the skimmer net from the hooks on the fence.

"Well...shiat." Thelma slapped at the water and grabbed the soggy pack. She frowned up at Sydney. "Who are you?"

"That's Dana's daughter, who doesn't need to be hearing your dirty mouth."

Thelma squinted at Sydney with mascara running down her face. "You home-schooled?"

Sydney shook her head. "No, ma'am."

"Then I'm sure you've heard worse."

"Yes, ma'am," Sydney said with a smile.

"You hear how she speaks to me, Alexandra? It's with respect. You need to pay attention."

Alex dumped the wiglet on the pool deck. "So do you."

Thelma pointed a gnarled finger at Sydney. "Your momma did a lot better job with you than Jean did with that jackass over there. If I could catch her, I'd beat the shit out of her. Don't you be followin' her example."

"Don't follow hers, either," Alex said with a grin. "You'll be drunk before noon and floating around in the pool like a polyester turd."

Sydney wanted to laugh, but Thelma was glaring at her.

"You see how she treats me?" Thelma said angrily. "She won't stay in this house because she knows if I find her sleeping I'll shave that pointed head of hers. I'd make my own wiglet out of her pelt. Now you two help this old woman on out of this pool."

Alex walked past Sydney and whispered, "You're gonna want to stay back. She'll drag you in on purpose."

Jean opened the lid to the potato salad and smiled. "This is Audrey's recipe, isn't it?"

Dana nodded and smiled as she leaned against the island.

"Does it upset you to talk about her?"

"Not anymore. I miss her, especially being back in the house," Dana said with a wan smile.

"I'm sure you do." Jean stared at Dana for a moment. "I still remember all those summer cookouts. Those were good times. Now that you're back, there'll be more. I know Alex is thrilled that you're in town."

Dana's face lit up. "It's so good to be around her again. I'm sure she doesn't realize it, but she just lifts me up."

"You do the same for her." Jean gazed out the kitchen windows. "She was in a bad way after the breakup. She and Vanessa parted amicably, but it still took a toll on her. You know what divorce does to you. Bad or good, it still hurts. Is Troy involved in Sydney's life?"

"No," Dana said with a sigh. "He was every bit the deadbeat my dad said he was. He's avoided child support by every means possible. After the divorce, I feared for a while that he would want to spend time with her. I just didn't know what kind of environment he would expose her to. When we split, he sort of went off the deep end and spent a lot of time in barrooms. Then he was just gone."

"That's a common story." Jean closed her eyes when the back door flew open. A few seconds later, Thelma rode in on her scooter blowing her horn.

"Can't stop to chat, gotta get myself cleaned up," Thelma said as she sped through, dripping all over the place with mascara under her eyes making her look like a raccoon.

Jean grinned sardonically. "Maybe she'll take a nap."

"Where's Dad?" Alex asked as she and Sydney walked in.

"He took the boat down to Kyle Satterwhite's house." Jean shrugged. "Something's wrong with the motor, it won't stay running. He'll be back shortly."

"The grill is hot, we're gonna put the meat on." Alex smiled at Sydney. "She's about to learn how to cook a Soileau rib."

"Oh, baby, pay close attention, those ribs are to die for." Dana closed her eyes. "I used to dream about those things. All of the Soileaus are great cooks, so soak up all the knowledge you can."

Sydney nodded. "I've already learned how not to light the grill."

"You and I are gonna have to talk about discretion," Alex said as she took a large tray of meat from the refrigerator. She turned to Jean. "The igniter's out again, and there was a little

Always Alex

tiny baby explosion when I lit it old school." Alex handed Sydney a pot with a lid on it. "You carry this."

Dana smiled. "Do y'all need my help?"

"Nope, we've got it," Sydney said before Alex could reply.

Jean watched the two walk out. "You've got yourself some competition for Alex's friendship," she said with a laugh.

Wade returned right as Alex was bringing in the food off the grill. He gave Dana a big hug and complimented her on Sydney. Then he announced, "Julia Satterwhite is gonna come down in a little while to play some volleyball in the pool. I figured Sydney would want someone her age to hang out with."

Jean frowned at him. "We don't have a volleyball set."

"We do now because I stopped off at the hardware store and picked one up." Wade slapped Alex on the shoulder. "This one is gonna be putting it up after lunch."

"Yay me. No ribs for you, Dad."

The food was set up buffet-style. Everyone made his or her plate and was about to sit at the table when Thelma wheeled in wearing a scarf tied around her head looking like a gypsy. She rolled right up to the table and stared expectantly at Jean, who left her food behind and made Thelma a plate.

"Mrs. Thelma, it's good to see you," Dana said politely.

"You've made a fine-looking woman. Got yourself some breasts now. You used to be flat as a board up there."

Alex sucked her teeth and glared when she caught Thelma's eye.

Dana bit her lip to keep from laughing.

Thelma stared at her plate when Jean set it in front of her. "Now, Jean, you know I can't eat ribs with my old teeth."

"They're very tender, Momma, just pick the meat off with your fork."

"Sydney, do you like to fish?" Wade asked.

"Yes, sir, I—"

"Jean, where's my drink?" Thelma asked.

"I'll get it," Alex said as she stood. "What do you want, Maw Maw—tea, Coke, or gasoline?"

"Coke." Thelma waited until Alex was just about to pour the soda and said, "No, tea." Alex pursed her lips and poured the tea instead. When she set the glass beside Thelma, she frowned at it. "I think I'd prefer lemonade."

Jean stared at her. "Oh, but you're in a cantankerous mood today."

Dana hid behind her napkin and laughed silently.

"Sydney, you were saying before you were interrupted?" Jean said with a smile.

"I used to—"

"This ice tastes like fish."

Jean clamped her lips together tightly before asking, "Sydney, have you ever seen a show called *Mama's Family*?"

Sydney smiled and nodded.

"Well, I'm about to go Eunice on her butt if she opens that mouth again."

Wade chuckled. "I do love Eunice." He waved a hand. "Go ahead and answer the question, honey."

"I like to fish," Sydney blurted out and glanced at Thelma.

Wade passed the bread to Dana. "We'll have to go sometime. I used to take your mom and Alex out to—"

"People's tails are ugly, that's why God covered 'em up with hair."

Jean slammed her hand down on the table. "Momma!"

Dana completely lost it. She nearly gagged herself when she inhaled part of the napkin she was holding over her mouth. Sydney did her best not to laugh but cracked up after she got over the initial shock. Wade continued eating like he hadn't heard a thing, and Alex sat with her hand over her face as Jean went Eunice on Thelma.

Chapter 9

Alex watched Sydney play volleyball with Julia in the pool. Her dad had made a good choice inviting Julia over. She was a great kid with a gregarious personality, and she and Sydney seemed to hit it off immediately.

Alex stretched out in her chaise lounge. "Are you ever going to quit laughing?"

"I can't stop." Dana sniffed and wiped her eyes. "I was looking directly at your mother when Thelma blurted out the hairy tail thing, and at first, she was totally stricken with shock, then her eyes rolled up in her head. And that statement was so horrifically random. What on earth made her think of something like that?"

Alex chuckled despite herself. "Vanessa and I were together three years before I brought her home for a visit. It took me that long to prep her for what she would face. Maw Maw pulled a fast one again like she did with my uncle. She was so nice and polite, Vanessa thought I was cruel for making fun of a sweet old lady. The very next day, Maw Maw offered Vanessa one of her Little Debbie cakes, and Vanessa turned it down, saying it was too fattening. Vanessa never heard the end of that. Maw Maw followed her around saying things like, 'So you think I'm fat, well, you ain't got no ass.'" Alex grinned. "Vanessa really didn't. I don't know how she sat for long periods of time."

"Does Thelma still call up the owls?"

"Yeah," Alex said with a laugh. "Y'all should stay until it at least gets dark, so Sydney can witness that."

Dana reached over and squeezed Alex's arm gently. "I know she made you mad, but that's the hardest laugh I've had in a long time."

"I think you just admitted that you haven't been happy in a while."

Caught off guard, Dana's smile slipped from her face. "I've had my ups and downs. The last few months have been a downer." She looked away and said, "Some of my wishes didn't come true."

"Mine didn't, either. I guess that's what we get for putting faith in pennies at the bottom of a septic tank." Alex smiled wistfully. "Barbier Point was suffocating me, and I thought if I could get out, I'd find everything that would make me happy."

Dana gazed at her. "What were you looking for?"

"The same thing you were—escape, love, someone to fill the gap that all of us are born with. The place that can only be filled by that one we truly connect with."

"You always had a way of putting words to what I feel. I wish I could keep you with me all the time to translate the words my heart whispers that I can't get to cross my lips. Why is it that we can connect, but we can't seem to do it with others we're in relationships with? Or did you? Did Vanessa find those hidden places?"

The reflection of the water danced in Alex's eyes as she turned and stared at it. "She and I were never that close, but for a long time, I tried to make myself believe that we were. I got to the point that I could no longer overlook how different we were. She's a good woman, she deserves the very best. I just couldn't…" Alex sighed. "Now I can't find the words."

"She didn't know you because you didn't trust her enough to truly reveal yourself?"

"I trusted her with everything else, but I didn't believe she could understand me. We just didn't commune on that level." Alex leaned back in her chair and put a hand behind her head. "Maybe what I want is a fantasy. Mom and Dad are opposites, but they work. Every now and then, I run across a couple, though, and they have it, you can see it. There was this couple Vanessa and I were friends with, they'd been together for twenty years. They still looked at each other like no one else existed."

Dana smiled. "Of course, you asked them what their secret was."

"Yes, I did," Alex said with a grin. "They gave me the same excuse all long-term couples give—communication, trust, commitment—but neither of them could explain the connection. They just had it, and the rest came easy." Alex caught the ball when it came soaring her way and threw it back in the pool.

"I want that," Dana said with a nod. "I want my feet to leave the ground and never touch down. I know what you're looking for because I've searched, too. I met a wonderful man a few years ago, good-looking, great sense of humor, stable, one of those guys that's really grounded. He had all the makings of a great catch, and I found myself staring at him over dinner one night wondering what was wrong with me because as much as I tried, I felt nothing. Did we miss the bus? Were we busy with someone else when the right one came by?"

Dana got up and went after the ball when it flew past them. Alex chewed the inside of her cheek, inwardly cursing irony. They were both searching for the same thing, and Alex felt she knew where to find it. The woman who she believed would fill the empty pocket in her soul stared right through her without ever noticing she would fit perfectly.

"That's mine, I called it." Dana lunged with her net, but Sydney was faster and snared the firefly. "Oh! You cheat!"

"You gotta be quick, old-timer," Sydney taunted as she put her bug in the jar Julia held. "Our jar is lighting up, and the one Alex is holding only has a glimmer."

"Don't let her rattle you, Dana. We've got this, we are master hunters." Alex caught a firefly in her net and yelled. "Ha!"

Dana grabbed their jar and got ready to open the lid when Jean yelled, "Time!"

"Well," Alex said with a smile. "We were once great hunters. Let our captives free."

Dana opened the jar and watched the lightning bugs, as she'd always called them, fly into a dusky sky as Alex freed her catch from the net. She bumped Alex with her hip. "We're still good. There's plenty of hunting years left in us."

Alex enjoyed the physical contact a little too much and moved away with a soft laugh. "Okay, Maw Maw, call in your feathered friends."

"Yoohoo, owls," Thelma called out drolly.

"Oh, come on, Mrs. Thelma, make them come," Julia pleaded.

"I'll call them for you and Sydney," Thelma said. "Don't sit near Alex because I've talked to a couple of them, and they have some business to attend to with her." She inhaled deeply and coughed. Once she cleared her throat, she began to make noises that sounded like an owl.

"She's so talented," Alex whispered as she offered Dana a chair.

It took a little while, but as everyone sat quietly on the patio, hoots began in the distance. "One night, I sat out here and called in a UFO," Thelma whispered seriously. "It looked like a big cigar with lights all around it."

"That was a jet, Momma."

Thelma pointed a finger at Jean. "Hush you, you're gonna scare the owls away." She made another call, and a few seconds later, the responding hoot was closer.

"I hope the monkey-sounding ones come," Julia said softly. "Those are my favorites."

Dana leaned close to Alex and whispered, "Are owls' tails ugly?"

"We'll know if they're covered with hair," Alex said just as quietly.

Thelma continued to hoot with results. She made varying noises that caused Sydney and Julia to laugh. Dana wondered if the owls did really think she was one of them or if they were simply curious to discover what creature was mimicking them. A shrill scream came from the tops of the trees above them.

Alex leaned closed to Sydney. "Now this is top-notch entertainment you won't find in New Orleans. I dare you to ask her if she's seen Bigfoot."

"I heard that, you jackass. I grew up near Honey Island Swamp, I've seen things that'd make your hair curl," Thelma snapped. "When I was a girl, I saw a fearsome creature outside my window one night."

"Were you drinking then?"

"Alex," Jean warned with a laugh.

A loud snore rang out. "Now that's a wild pig," Thelma said. "Sometimes, I call those in, too."

"That was Dad."

"Huh?"

"Go back to sleep, honey," Jean said as she patted his arm.

"Told ya, wild pig," Thelma said smugly.

Dana stretched her arm out on the back of Alex's chair, her hand rested on Alex's shoulder. She'd always been the touchy type. When they were kids, she'd often sit close to Alex so that she could toy with her hair. Alex knew it was an innocent sign of affection, but the warmth it stirred brought the reality she was trying to avoid crashing in. Her feelings had never changed for Dana. It was more than a childhood crush, and emotions would grow stronger unless she could find a way to bring them under control.

After they dropped Julia off at her house, Sydney and Dana drove Alex home. Sydney waited in the truck as Dana walked Alex to her door. The fireflies had seemed to follow them and danced in the dark shadows.

"I had a wonderful time, and I know Sydney did, too. Thank you so much for inviting us over." Dana wrapped her arms around Alex's waist and held her snugly. "I don't think you realize what you do for me."

"I can say the same," Alex said. "We'll have to do this again. Maybe the boat will be running by next weekend and we can take it out."

Dana released her and took a step back. "I'll look forward to that. Good night."

"Good night," Alex called out as Dana walked away.

When Dana climbed into the truck, Sydney shifted into reverse and managed to back up without stalling. Dana smiled. "You're picking this up so fast." She waved at Alex, who was standing in her doorway watching.

"Do you have a crush on her?"

Dana whipped her head around. "Why would you ask that?"

"Because I've never seen you be that touchy-feely with your other friends."

Dana shrugged. "I guess I always have. Instead of a bromance, it's a galmance. Hey, you and Julia seemed to really hit it off."

Sydney nodded. "I like her, she's a lot of fun, somebody I could hang with. We might go see a movie sometime."

"I don't know how I feel about that."

Sydney sounded surprised when she asked, "Why?"

"Because the closest theater is almost an hour away in another town."

"Mom, I'm seventeen and she's eighteen."

"I know how old you are, Sydney, I gave birth to you, remember?"

"So cut the umbilical cord already."

"Watch that tone. I didn't say no, but if you push, you know that's what the answer will be. I need to think about it."

Sydney started to say something else and blew out a breath instead. Dana knew she was ticked off and in a way empathized with her. She knew what it was like to have her wings clipped. They made the ride home in silence. When they drove around the back of the house, the headlights of the truck swept across the yard, and for a split second, they illuminated a white picket fence.

"Would you take the dishes inside?" Dana asked as she unclipped her seat belt.

Sydney's "sure" lacked enthusiasm.

Dana sat back and looked at her. "You've driven around New Orleans, you can handle the trip to Houma. You can go to the movies. And yes, sometimes, I forget you're seventeen."

Sydney smiled. "Thanks, Mom."

"When you were born, you needed everything from me. I had to get used to that. You used to want me to hold you and my affection all the time, then you changed, but I never did. The instinct and the desire to nurture and protect is still there, and it always will be."

"We're gonna hug now, aren't we?" Sydney said with resignation.

Dana stuck out her bottom lip. "I want to."

"You're so goofy," Sydney said with a laugh as she wrapped her arms around Dana's neck. "Sometimes, I still want you to hold me, but I'll let you know when that's necessary."

Dana grinned. "I'll be prepared."

They climbed out of the truck, and Sydney took the dishes inside while Dana walked over to where the fence had been installed. Beneath the moonlight, she could see the freshly tilled earth in neat rows inside the confines of the picket fence. There was a gate and above it an arch. It looked just like the picture she'd seen. She knew it meant something to her father, and it was special to her because it was a token of his affection.

Chapter 10

"Have you talked to Dana?" Jean asked as she put the finishing touches on dinner.

"No, she started that new job, and I'm sure she's tired."

Jean watched Alex slice the bread, noting the tension lines marring her forehead. "You looked like you were having a wonderful time with her the other day."

Alex nodded. "I did."

"Sydney seems to be fond of you."

"Yeah, I like her, too," Alex said with a slight smile.

"I bought a huge roast today, saw it on sale, and had to grab it. I think I'll cook it on… You were in love with her as a girl, and you still are."

Alex's gaze slowly rose to meet her mother's.

Jean sliced her hands through the air. "I had to put it out there. It's like a big white love elephant that no one acts like they notice…maybe your father hasn't. He's pretty clueless most of the time about things like that. Alexandra, talk to me!"

"The point is moot, Momma."

"Then tell me how you feel, what you're thinking. It took you so long to pull out of the funk you were in after Vanessa left, and now you look like you're in it again."

Alex set the knife down. "It's true," she said without meeting Jean's gaze. "I've always loved her, but I also know the facts, which is she's a straight woman who can only see me as her best friend."

Jean shook her head. "It seems like so much more than that. She can't keep her hands off of you, she—"

"Please don't," Alex said quietly. "Dana has always been affectionate, that's just her way. I struggle to not read too much into what she does or says because it gives me false hope. If I'm going to survive having her back in my life, I have to accept the truth."

Jean came around the counter and wrapped her arms around Alex. "The truth sucks."

Alex smiled and nodded. "Yes, it does."

"Maybe you shouldn't spend a lot of time with her."

"That's going to be hard, she's my best friend."

The tires of Thelma's scooter squeaked on the kitchen floor as she rolled in and skidded to a stop. "Guess what I just read? In Aussie slang, freckle means anus. Jean, you've got buttholes all over your face."

Jean flicked Alex on the ear. "I'll never forgive you for buying her that weird fact magazine subscription."

Dana carefully pulled two hydrangeas from the trunk of her car and set them on the driveway. She'd hoped to spend a little time in the garden each night after work, but training with Lisa was mentally exhausting. For the last three evenings, she came home, skipped dinner, and took long baths with a glass of wine. She intended to repeat the process that evening, but as she passed the hardware store, she was compelled to have a look at the nursery. Dana hauled the plants she picked over to the garden and set them on either side of the gate. They weren't as large as the mature hydrangeas in the photo, but with a little time and care, they would be. She was unable to find a clematis, but the clerk informed her there was a much larger nursery ten miles out of town that would probably have one.

"What possessed you to choose those plants and place them there?"

Dana turned and watched as Daniel drew closer. "I saw a photo of Grandma's garden. I'd like to replicate it."

A sliver of a smile crept across Daniel's face. "That would be lovely."

"Think back to what it looked like. Tell me what she had planted in there."

Daniel closed his eyes and placed both hands atop his cane. "Give me a moment."

Dana studied his face that had gone soft with age. He was still handsome, though his eyebrows needed a trim. They reminded her of two gray and black caterpillars. The afternoon breeze ruffled his royal blue and white shirt and sent the scent of his cologne her way.

"Snap beans grew on the fence. There were tomatoes, eggplant, squash, cucumbers…I remember a watermelon or two." Daniel smiled. "Strawberries. She used to have me gather up pine straw to protect them from the frost. In the corners, she planted flowers," he said as he opened his eyes. "I don't know what they were, but they drew butterflies, very bushy and colorful."

"How do you remember all of that?"

"Because she made me weed it, and so I wouldn't pull the wrong thing, she taught me what each plant was." Daniel flashed a genuine smile then. "And I ate a lot while I worked, especially the berries. Momma claimed I was worse than a crow. Memory is a funny thing. I can see that part of the past so clearly, but I can't recall something I've done less than an hour ago."

Dana smiled. "What else do you remember about your childhood?"

Daniel clamped his lips together and breathed in through his nose as his eyes narrowed. "I hated wearing shoes. I remember going to school one day and hiding a pair under the shrubs. I told my teachers that I didn't have any. My plan worked for a few days until the principal spoke to my mother at church one Sunday. She was completely humiliated and furious with me." One of his bushy eyebrows rose. "I didn't care much for clothes back then, either. In the summer, I wore a pair of shorts, and that was it. My skin was as dark as a ripe berry. I felt so alive then with the grass beneath my bare feet and the sun on my back. I could run for miles. You used to like to run, too. You sprinted right off the end of the Guilbeaus' dock at a party."

Dana laughed. "I'd forgotten about that story. How old was I?"

Daniel shook his head with another real smile. "Four, I think. I was holding you as I spoke to someone and you were squirming, so I set you down and took my eyes off you for just a second. I heard the clack of your little sandals against the wood. I chased after you and watched in horror as you launched yourself into the air without the least bit of hesitation. I went in right after you wearing the white pair of slacks that your mother insisted I wear to match her outfit. That proved most unfortunate as I carried you out of the bay. The material was a tad revealing. You were totally unrepentant and wanted to go again."

Dana and Daniel turned when Sydney pulled in and parked next to Dana's car. "She's driving it on her own now," Daniel said with delight. "I'm so proud of her."

"I am, too."

"When did you learn to drive a stick?"

"Alex taught me on Dune Road when it was still dirt. She was so patient because I must've stalled that car a million times."

Daniel turned to Dana, his expression solemn. "Do you know what she is?"

Dana felt her protective hackles rise. "I know she is one of the most genuine people I've ever met."

Daniel stared at her for a moment as Sydney approached. "She's a good woman."

Dana blinked as she watched Sydney give her grandfather a hug. He hugged her back without the least bit of hesitation and with genuine affection.

"Hey, Mom."

"Hey…baby. How was work?"

"Busy, and I'm starving. There was no time to eat today." Sydney winced. "On my breaks, I propped my feet up because they ached so bad."

"You need proper shoes," Daniel said as he gazed at the orange Converse on Sydney's feet. "Definitely something with a strong arch support."

"You should wear your running shoes until this weekend when we can shop for something else," Dana suggested.

"Let's go inside and see what Clara has prepared for dinner. I think it may be pork chops," Daniel said as he patted Dana on the back.

Dana soaked in a tub of tepid water since Sydney had bathed first and nearly drained the hot water heater. She stared at the glass of red wine as she thought about the conversation with Daniel, the hug he gave Sydney, and the pat on her back. Her defenses had been high upon her return; she expected recrimination from the cold aloof man she'd resented for years. She was afraid to drop her guard and let him in again, but there was a part of her that wanted to. She knew Daniel didn't have a lot of years left, and if they could spend that time at peace, if he could be the father she knew before Mary's loss, at least one of her wishes would come true.

She smiled as she sipped her wine and thought of the so-called wishing well. Now she understood why most of her wishes had turned to shit. Apparently, Alex's one consistent wish, the one she'd never reveal, didn't come true, either. From what she'd said the day they spent together, Dana gathered that Alex had been wishing for that special one just like she had. She wanted happiness for Alex, but at the same time, she was selfishly pleased that Alex was also single. She didn't like to share her best friend, she never had.

Alex lay on her side staring out the window of her bedroom watching the fireflies dance in the tree line. The steady whir of a box fan lulled her as she contemplated her stupidity. On impulse, she'd called Collette Crochet and asked her to dinner Friday night. The logic was simple—occupy herself with an available woman who would take up her time and temporarily take her mind off Dana.

How tragic it was to realize that her feelings for Dana had never truly gone away but lain dormant like a disease waiting for the catalyst to spread like wildfire. She was wracked with a pain there was no pill for. Nothing eased the ache. Like an addict, she knew she'd seek out the source of her torment time and time again.

Chapter 11

"Hey, how was your week?"

"Good," Alex lied as she cradled her phone on her shoulder and fastened her jeans. "How was yours?"

"Can I just tell you that Lisa Beaudreaux has one big fat snooker for you?"

Alex groaned and laughed. "She's made that quite clear. Everyone at work knows that I refuse to be in an exam room alone with her."

"What're you doing? I hear you shuffling around."

Alex tried to sound upbeat as she said, "I'm getting dressed to go to dinner with a woman I know."

Dana was silent for a second or two. "I thought you said you weren't ready to date."

"This is…kind of a friendly date, not really a date kind of thing."

"Oh, so it's a platonic thing."

"Sometimes."

Dana was quiet again, then inhaled sharply. "You have a fuck buddy!"

"She's a friend with benefits."

"Who is she?"

"A pharmaceutical rep that travels a lot. I don't see her very often," Alex said as she walked into her bedroom and opened her closet. "Red or blue shirt?"

"Red, it goes well with your coloring. Why are you even bothering to get dressed?"

Alex chose the red one and slipped it on while juggling the phone. "It's not all sex. Sometimes, we just go have dinner and talk."

"I'm so jealous," Dana admitted with a laugh that didn't sound genuine to either of them.

"What're you doing tonight?"

"I was going to see if you wanted to have a drink."

"How about tomorrow night?" Alex ran her hands through her hair and just gave up on doing anything with it.

"That sounds great. Call me."

"I will. Thanks for the clothing advice."

"Go have fun."

When the call ended, Dana looked at her watch. If she hurried, she could get to the nursery before it closed and pick up the clematis and a few vegetable plants. She grabbed her keys and jogged downstairs.

"Clara, I'm gonna run to the store, do you need anything?"

"No, dear, but thank you. Where's Sydney?"

"She took an extra shift when someone called in sick. She'll be home by nine."

Clara looked up from the crossword puzzle she was working at the kitchen table. "I'll keep dinner warm for her in case she wants to eat."

"Thank you."

Dana jogged out to her car and climbed in. As she drove out of the driveway, she wondered what it would be like to go on a date with a woman. Men naturally took the lead, but she was curious as to whom assumed that role between women. She figured in Alex's case, it was her. Dana smiled as she imagined Alex and her chivalrous nature. She'd be the type to open doors and initiate the good night kiss, maybe more if the evening went well. Her smile faded as an image of Alex being intimate with a woman flashed through her mind. A feeling of disquiet settled in the pit of her stomach.

We went for hours. Sex with a woman is work! But, oh, the orgasms. She played my body like a fiddle. I kept hitting those high notes if you know what I mean.

Dana shook her head to dispel Lisa's voice from her mind. "Hours…wow."

There had been a time that Dana had been tempted to explore that side of the fence. But then, Mardi Gras made people do crazy things like show their body parts in public for a string of plastic beads. She and a group of girlfriends had wandered down Bourbon Street with the foolish goal of having a drink in every bar. Sydney was safe with a sitter, Troy was off with his friends, and Dana felt she could really let herself be free for a few hours.

They wandered into a bar, not really paying attention to where they were. The music was good, and the whole group of friends went onto the dance floor. One minute Dana was dancing with someone familiar, and the next, she wasn't. There were so many people packed into the small area, it seemed that they moved as one. Dana found herself pinned against a woman who set her hands on her waist. Dana felt them slide down her hips. "You don't really belong in here, do you?" the woman said against her ear.

"I'm old enough," Dana retorted lamely, her addled mind failing to grasp the meaning.

"You're really cute," the woman said with a laugh. "I'm Samantha, you can call me Sam."

Dana felt Sam's fingers against the skin of her back as they crept beneath her shirt. The meaning of Sam's statement clicked then, but Dana didn't pull away, entranced by the hypnotic beat of the music, the body against hers, and the touch that stirred something within. Sam's hands slipped down Dana's backside, a thigh slid between her legs. Dana's hands rested on Sam's arms, and she unconsciously gripped the moist skin. She was married and knew the titillating feelings were taboo, but she couldn't seem to find the will to pull away. And then a hand grabbed her shoulder and pulled hard; the spell Sam cast was broken as one of her friends dragged her away. Later and sober, Dana thought back on the encounter and decided that alcohol was the reason for the loss of her inhibitions. But on nights when Troy wanted sex and she didn't, she allowed the fantasy of what might've happened to play out, amazed by how much it turned her on.

Dana shook her head when she realized that she was sitting in the parking lot of the nursery, and she didn't remember how she got there. Her hands felt clammy against the wheel, and arousal coursed through her veins. She blew out a breath.

"...so when I finally got into his office, I hogtied him and stuck an apple in his mouth. Then I spanked him with a boat paddle."

Alex slowly lowered her fork. "You did what?"

"I was just making sure you were still with me. Your eyes have glazed over a few times," Collette said with a patient smile.

"I'm so sorry. You have my full attention now."

Collette smiled, and with a sexy timbre asked, "Will I have it later?"

Alex stared at the beautiful woman sitting across the table from her, images of past couplings filling her mind. Her hands filled with Collette's blond hair, her mouth doing intensely pleasurable things to her body. Parts of Alex's anatomy responded, but her stubborn heart cried no.

Collette gazed at her as she sipped her wine. "I see indecision in those brown eyes."

Alex's expression was pained. "I have a problem."

"Well, I'm sure there's a pill or a cream for it, sugar."

Alex laughed. "Not that kind."

Collette sighed and set her glass down. "Aw, hell, have you fallen in love with someone? Do you know how hard it is to find a casual partner that's disease-free? Alex, you didn't have to take me to dinner to break it off, you could've told me over the phone."

"That's not why I called you." Alex pinched the bridge of her nose. "This is so complicated."

Collette motioned for their server and ordered a brownie à la mode. "If I'm not going to be getting your sugar tonight, then I'll get it elsewhere. Talk to me."

Alex drummed her fingers on the table. "Okay, here's the condensed version. I fell in love with my childhood best friend, but she never knew. I went off to college, she moved away and got married, eventually divorced. Now we're both back in Barbier Point, and after all the time that has passed, we're still just as close as we used to be. She always held a special place in my heart, but now I realize that she owns the whole thing. I can't stay away from her, but I can't have her, either."

Collette pursed her lips and nodded. "Well then, the answer is very simple. Tell her how you feel."

Alex shook her head emphatically. "That's not simple, so not simple."

"Not emotionally, no." Collette released a moan when the server set her dessert in front of her. "Sex in a bowl." She picked up her spoon and smiled at Alex. "One of two things will happen when you tell her. The best, obviously, would be for her to admit she has her own unrequited feelings, but face it, that normally doesn't happen. So the most logical assumption is she'll be shocked, maybe even a little distant until she can come to terms with it. This will be painful to you, but at least you've purged your feelings. This kind of thing happens all the time. It happened to me, although she wasn't a childhood love. That's exactly how I dealt with it, and now I'm over her."

"Well, what happened? Tell me." Alex pulled the dessert away from Collette. "I need details."

"You're gonna get kicked in the tail if you don't give that back." Collette snatched the bowl from Alex and took a big bite. Her eyes rolled up in her head as she swallowed. "Sometimes, ice cream is better than a woman…sometimes."

"Could you have your oral orgasm and talk at the same time?"

Collette waved her spoon. "Here it is, condensed version, as you say. We worked together, she was straight, but I fell for her anyway. She made me laugh, we had a ton in common, she was a stylish dresser. Oh, my God, that woman could accessorize. We did everything together, and the whole time, I pined away for her until I couldn't stand it any longer. So one day, I told her exactly how I felt." Collette took another bite and stared at her spoon. "You get really stupid when you're wrapped up like that and start believing that looks and touches mean more than they actually do. She gave me a look that night that couldn't be interpreted as anything but disgust. Then she went to the office the next day and told our boss, who transferred me to the sales route I'm on now. My feelings of love quickly dissipated, and now I hate that bitch. End of story."

Collette scooted the bowl across the table. "You can have the cherry because, sweetie, the chance of getting hers is very slim."

Later that evening, Alex did some serious soul searching while sitting on her deck with a carton of rocky road. Collette was wrong about one thing—ice cream was not better than a woman…ever. But lactose intolerance had a lot to do with that. Alex knew that she was not going to take Collette's advice, but she had no idea how she was going to learn to cope with the feelings that grew stronger every time she was around Dana.

Chapter 12

"The dirt is so soft, you don't need a trowel to make a hole," Dana said as she dug with her hand. She picked up one of the tomato plants, gave the container a squeeze, and pulled the plant out by the stem. "They're good and root-bound, that means when we get them in the soil, they'll really take off. You squeeze the root ball a little just to get them loose, then you set it in the hole, which should be the same depth of the container." Dana demonstrated and packed the earth tightly around the new planting.

Sydney, who had the weekend off and volunteered to help, did the exact same thing on her row. "How's that?"

Dana slapped her on the shoulder. "Excellent job, baby."

Sydney frowned at the dirty handprint on her shirt. "Keep your mitts to yourself, Mom."

"Oh, come on. You're kneeling in the soil. It's good to get grimy every now and then," Dana said with a smile. "There's something very therapeutic about putting your hands in the earth, isn't there?"

"I don't want the earth inside my clothes. Oh, gross! What is that?"

Dana turned and looked at the large insect Sydney was pointing at. She thumped it and sent it flying through the slats of the fence and held up her arms like a referee confirming a touchdown. "Score one for Mom. That was a mole cricket.

The front part of their body looks kinda like a mole with the little digging legs and the back looks like a cricket, but they fly."

"Do they bite?"

Dana shook her head as she picked up another plant. "Not that I know of. They'll tear up a lawn, though, because they eat the grass roots."

Sydney dug a new hole in her row. "Where'd you learn about this stuff?"

"I read. It's a marvelous thing, you learn all sorts of stuff."

Sydney snorted. "You need to get a life."

"And you need to crack a book."

"I'm an honor student, I must be doing something right."

Dana smiled. "I'm not knocking that, but maybe instead of texting and talking on your phone all night, you could read something that would broaden your mind."

"That's the only time I get to talk to Leighton. She's working this summer, too."

"What's she doing?"

"Answering phones at her dad's office."

Dana watched Sydney out of the corner of her eye. "She's a really sweet girl. I miss her."

"I do, too," Sydney said somberly. "Her dad told her if she finished the year with straight A's, he might let her visit me this summer. Leighton kept up her end of the bargain, so we're waiting to see if he'll keep his."

"I think it's really cool how you two have maintained your friendship with so much distance between you."

Sydney glanced at Dana as she packed dirt around one of the plants. "Just like you and Alex."

"Well, some friends you keep forever, no matter what."

"Right, and Leighton will always be mine."

"I will be, too," Dana said with a warm smile. "I know there are some things you don't want to discuss with me because I'm your mom, but you know me to be very open-minded. I will always love you regardless of—" Dana inhaled sharply and grabbed the crotch of her shorts.

Sydney's brow furrowed for a second, then she grinned. "Your balls finally drop?"

Dana's eyes were wide as her jaw worked, and she finally spat out, "There's something in my shorts, it's trying to burrow into my underwear."

Sydney scrambled to her feet when Dana, still grasping the front of her shorts, jumped up. "What is it?" Sydney demanded.

"It's really hard…I think…I think it's a mole cricket." Dana shuddered and made a terrible face. "I feel its legs digging on my skin."

"Pull your pants down!"

"I can't! These are running shorts with the underwear made into them, and Dad is sitting right over there. Syd, you gotta go in and get it while I hold it."

"Momma, no!" Sydney said with disgust as she backed up and destroyed part of a row.

"I can't let it go! It'll get into my underwear, then it'll…oh, my God, I can't go there. They burrow," Dana squeaked out. "Help me."

"I can't touch that thing and your thing!" Sydney took another step back.

"Fine! Get in front of me so I can pull my shorts down."

Sydney moved between her mother and her grandfather's line of vision. The garden fence did allow them some privacy as Dana squirmed around behind her. "Grandpa's looking."

"Just stay where you are. Oh…my God." Dana groaned as she bumped into Sydney. "Oh…it's touching my…oh…no, the legs…feel so…icky. It's…coming…it's coming…it's…oh…to the left, you bastard. It's…coming…oh…oh…yes!"

Sydney sounded repulsed when she said, "I feel so dirty right now."

"*You* feel dirty? I'm digging legs outta my underwear. Stay still, it's stuck. The thing has barbs."

"Where is the rest of it?" Sydney asked with alarm.

"Under my foot, I'm crushing it."

Sydney giggled. "It's probably already dead. It was in your shorts after all."

"You want it in your butt crack?"

"Alex, hand me a flathead screwdriver," Wade said as he crawled around the inside of the boat.

"A fathead with a flathead," Thelma quipped from where she sat close by on her scooter.

"You must be very bored if you're sitting out here watching us clean the boat," Alex said as she handed her father the screwdriver.

"Pestering you two is a lot more fun than staring at the boob tube. There's not a lot to do when you're old and dying. I ain't one to knit or crochet. But I have been doing some reading. Do you shave?" Thelma asked as she lit up a cigarette.

"Do you see hair on my legs?"

Thelma pointed to Alex's shorts. "I mean down *there*."

"What is your preoccupation with pubic hair lately?"

"There's a big ol' ad in my magazine. They're selling something called a 'painless Brazilian.' I ain't never met anyone from Brazil, but I read all the fine print on the ad to find out why they're supposed to be painful. Come to find out, they were talking about cooter hair. That must be the new thing, no fur. I was gonna ask Sydney about it the other day because she's a young'un, but your mother lost her mind on me."

"Ah," Alex said with a nod. "Now the 'people's tails are ugly' comment makes sense."

"Well, they are. I don't understand why y'all want to rip all the hair off of 'em. Are you up with the times?"

Alex shook her head as she dropped the screwdriver into the boat. "My private area is private."

"I ain't seen mine in years, my ol' stomach's done flopped over on it. There's probably a train wreck down there."

"Dear God," Alex heard her father mumble from inside the boat.

Alex wiped her brow as she replaced a taillight on the boat trailer. "Can we talk about something else, Maw Maw?"

Thelma nodded and blew out a plume of smoke. "I think Viagra is evil. Sure, a woman likes that ol' ugly stick when she's first married. Then it becomes a nuisance popping up everywhere, and she spends all the time trying to get away from it. The good Lord designed them dicks to stop working when a man gets into his later years for a reason—so a woman can have her rest. And now men have made themselves a pill so they can keep right on pestering with that thing."

"That's a mighty piece of valuable insight," Alex said. "I'll store that in the file I have marked as 'don't give a shit.'"

"I should call an owl down on your ass for being so smart-mouthed. You were a sweet child. I don't know what happened to you."

"You happened." Alex stretched out the hose and prepared to wash the boat.

Thelma chuckled. "I trained you right then."

"Alex, I need the socket wrench and a five-eight."

"He can probably fit his whole dick in that," Thelma said with a loud guffaw.

"At least I can see mine," Wade shot back, his voice sounding muffled.

"Alexandra, that's one thing you ain't gotta trifle with, you being a lesbian and all. I just wonder where you and Andrew got that came from, probably Wade's side of the family. I did have an uncle who got caught carrying a purse once, but he stole it."

Alex ignored Thelma and added water to her soap bucket. But Thelma was in the mood to spar and went for Alex's jugular. "I seen you making eyes at Dana the other day. I hope you know you don't stand a chance with her. She's a woman that's—"

Wade popped up like a gopher. "Shut up and go on, Thelma. If you don't want your cigarette and booze well to run dry, then you'll clamp that yap of yours shut and drive off. I've had enough of listening to you."

Wade rarely ever showed his temper. The only time anyone really knew he was angry was when he stalked off. But Thelma realized she'd gone too far when he threatened her lifeline. She scowled as she whirled her scooter around and headed to the house.

"Don't ever take anything that woman says to heart," Wade said as he disappeared from view again. "One of the latches in here has come loose, otherwise I don't see any problems with it, aside from being dirty. I picked you up a new ski rope. This boat is ready to cruise just in time for Memorial Day weekend. I think you should give Dana a call, and invite her and Sydney out on the lake."

Alex watched as Thelma rolled across the lawn and thumped a cigarette into the grass. "I'll do that right now." She walked a little distance away and called Dana as she'd promised. "Hey, what're you doing?"

"I just got out of the shower. Sydney and I shopped for some work shoes for her, then we did some gardening today."

"Dad and I are cleaning up the boat. Do you think she'd be interested in skiing tomorrow if she's off work?"

"She is off, and I'm sure she would. I'd definitely like to ride around in your boat. Are you still free for drinks tonight, or do you have another date?"

"Nope, I'm free," Alex said as she found some shade. "What did you have in mind?"

"A bottle of wine on Dune Road at sunset like we used to do as kids. Of course, then it was a wine cooler and you'd only let me have one sip."

"Sounds perfect," Alex said with a smile.

"I'll bring the wine and pick you up at six thirty."

Alex cleaned the boat inside and out, then went up to the

house where she found her mother in the kitchen. "Do you still have that small green cooler bag?"

Jean was staring at a cookbook. "Yes, it's in the cabinet inside the island."

Alex dug around until she found it. "Do you have French bread, cubed cheeses, crackers, and maybe a small portable dessert?"

Jean looked up from her book, her glasses perched on the tip of her nose. "Yes, I have bread and crackers, a block of cheese you can slice yourself. There's a multiple flavor cheesecake wheel in the freezer. When you go to the grocery store, do you actually get a cart and put things inside of it?"

A retort froze on the tip of Alex's tongue when she heard Thelma belting *Silver Wangs* on the front porch. "She's drunk as a skunk, isn't she?"

"Your father hurt her feelings when he yelled at her," Jean said with a sigh. "She came in and had me fetch her bottle of Mad Dog 20/20 from the back of the pantry. That's reserved for special emotional times, you know."

Alex got out the cheese and set it on the slicer. "Dad didn't yell, it was more like a well-deserved snap. She called him a fathead and insulted his penis."

"I kind of like it when she drinks that stanky dog wine. She sings, cries, and for just a little while before she passes out, she's kinda loving. I'm gonna put another bottle of that on the grocery list," Jean said as she made a notation, then looked at Alex. "Who are you going on a picnic with?"

"Dana and I are just going out to Dune Road to watch the sunset. She's bringing a bottle of wine, so I thought I should bring something to accompany it."

"Wine, cheese, a sunset, that sounds romantic. Do you know what you're doing?"

Alex nodded. "I've decided to put my heart in a box, lock it away."

"Baby, that doesn't work for anyone but your maw maw. What happens if Dana gets past your box?"

Alex reached into the freezer and pulled out the cheesecake. "Then I'll become just like Maw Maw, but I can't drink Mad Dog. Put some Jack Daniels on your shopping list."

The screen door on the front porch burst open, and Thelma arrived in the kitchen a few seconds later with mascara-stained cheeks. "Oh, Alex, I never meant to hurt your feelings, baby. I love you. I'd never really ask an owl to eat your face off. I'm sorry I said that about Dana, I just don't want you to get hurt." She threw her arms open wide. "Come here and let me love you."

Alex looked at Jean, who jerked her head toward Thelma. "Go," she mouthed.

Alex walked over and patted her on the hand. "It's okay, Maw Maw, I don't listen to half of the crap you say."

Thankful that she had not already bathed, Alex found her head in Maw Maw's bosom. It smelled of sweat, cigarettes, and wine, and there was a piece of a Little Debbie cake that stuck to Alex's face as Thelma squeezed her.

"I'm better now, you can let me go…please…let go."

"I'm really surprised they haven't paved this and built houses out here like they've done in the rest of the areas near the water," Dana said as she carefully dodged a pothole on Dune Road.

"Somebody that lives in Lafayette bought almost all of the property along here, and the rumor is they want to build some sort of nature retreat on it. That was years ago, though."

"I was telling Dad the other day that this was where you taught me to drive a stick. Do you remember that?" Dana asked with a smile.

Alex rubbed the back of her neck. "Yeah, it took me years to get over the whiplash."

"You did that to yourself cutting doughnuts in the dirt. You drove that car like a dune buggy."

"And that piece of crap lasted me through my first year of college. When it finally gave up the ghost, it was like losing a family member. I actually shed a tear when the tow truck drove off with it."

Dana glanced at Alex. "You went parking down here with Mark Lanoux. Did you really have sex with him? Tell me the truth."

"Oh, let's not go there," Alex said miserably as she looked out the window.

"C'mon, I'm your BFF, remember? He told everyone at school y'all did." Dana slowed down and parked at the end of the road. She turned off the ignition and looked at Alex. "Tell me."

Alex sighed long and loud. "We're gonna have to open the wine for this story."

"Oh, goodie, it's gonna be good," Dana said as she threw open her door.

"Trust me, it's not." Alex climbed out of the car and grabbed the cooler out of the backseat as Dana pulled two folding chairs from the trunk.

The strip of sand along the water's edge was narrow until they came to a spot jutting out a few feet into the water where they set up their chairs. Dana took out a corkscrew, opened the bottle of cabernet, and cursed. "I forgot the damn glasses."

"No biggie, we'll drink it right out of the bottle like we used to."

Dana took a swallow and handed it to Alex. "I believe you owe me a story."

"I need more. You're driving anyway." Alex lifted the bottle to her lips and drank before handing it back to Dana. "That is very tasty and smooth."

"Start talking."

"Okay, so we came down here and made out for like an hour. I wasn't into guys then, but I thought I should give them a try just to be sure. So I let him go to all the bases but home, then I decided that I was just going to do it. Mark undid his pants, and this thing flops out." Alex folded her arms and shuddered. "Dana, it was fucking huge, like porn star huge. It looked like an arm. I took one look at that thing and climbed into the front seat like I was running away from a big ugly-ass snake. There was no way I was going to let him get near me with it. So we made a deal. I told him he could tell his friends we did it if he would take me home. That's the last time I ever saw one of those in person, and I'm really happy about it."

Dana handed the bottle back to Alex with a laugh. "You deserve another drink."

"Damn right I do. He had the nerve to ask me for a blow job! The question alone made me gag."

Dana chuckled. "I remember all the lovesick horny boys that followed you around and the love notes they begged me to give to you."

"I think maybe I was sending off some sort of lesbian signal, and they all wanted the chance to flip me."

Dana shook her head and took the bottle back from Alex. "You were gorgeous, still are. Those smoky brown eyes are a knockout. I was always so jealous of them. I used to sit at the mirror for hours and try to make mine look like that. I can't tell you how many eye pencils and mascara I went through."

"You were pretty back then, but you didn't know it. I think you do now, you're a lot more confident." Alex looked away when Dana gazed at her intently. "This was a good idea. I think we're in for a pretty show."

"Yeah," Dana said with a sigh. "But I see dark clouds off to the southwest, we'll probably get rain tonight. Hey, how'd the date go?"

Alex shrugged. "We had a nice time. After dinner, Collette ordered this brownie—"

"How nice?" Dana asked with a slight edge in her tone, then released a goofy laugh. "I mean…did you…you know?"

"No." Alex kicked off her flip-flops and dug her toes into the sand. "We just talked and had dinner."

"So…it just ended with a kiss good night and no…wham-bam-thank-you-ma'am. Were you disappointed?"

"No. Collette was willing." Alex shrugged. "I just wasn't in the mood."

"But you kissed her good night?"

Alex reached over and took the bottle from Dana's hands. "What's with all the questions?"

"I'm…I'm curious," Dana said wide-eyed. "I've never had that kind of experience—you know, the casual thing. What happens if one of you develops feelings and the other doesn't?"

Alex shrugged and took a long drink. "I don't know. That never happened with us. We both know it can't be any more than it is. Collette lives somewhere in north Alabama. She's only in this area a couple times a month."

"So how did this thing begin?"

"I saw her one night when I was out with friends at a bar in Houma. There's quite a few lesbian couples that live in Barbier, by the way. I asked Collette to dance. Later on, she asked me back to her hotel, and I went. We had a great time and decided to get together again when she came into town with no strings. She's really a nice…" Alex fell silent when she noticed that Dana was looking at her like she'd kicked a puppy. "Is this grossing you out?"

"No, no. I'm fascinated. I'm learning things," Dana said as she turned and looked at the changing colors in the sky. "Nothing about you grosses me out."

"So did you say you were gardening?"

"Yeah." Dana scooted down in her chair and leaned her head against the back of it. "Sydney said that Dad asked what I liked to do, and she told him gardening. So he had a crew come in over the weekend, till up the ground, and build a fence around it to make a garden like his mother used to have. Then he went out and bought me all sorts of tools and gave me a gift certificate for plants so I could work in it. Last night, he talked to me, told me old stories about when I was a kid and when he was growing up." Dana held up a finger. "And he hugged Sydney."

"I need to have Clara bring him in, so I can see if he's had a stroke." Alex handed the bottle back to Dana.

"Right?" Dana shook her head and laughed. "That's not the man I knew. I keep waiting for him to morph into the berating, cold authoritarian I couldn't wait to get away from." Dana lowered her voice and imitated Daniel. "You don't self-analyze, you never stop and think, you just react. That's why you'll always have to have someone to tell you what to do. Like some dumb animal, you need to be led around by your nose."

Alex winked at her. "You sure proved him wrong. Life sometimes makes a person hard, then there's Maw Maw, who is just naturally a shit." Alex picked at the label on the wine. "It sounds like he's had a lot of time to think, and he's trying to make up for the past."

"I'm sure he is." Dana sighed and looked up at the sky as it began to turn pink and orange. "We'll end up having a talk, and I'll cry. All of my defenses will come tumbling down because I want so much for things to be like they were before Mary died. I want to hold on to my anger because it protects me, but I can feel it slipping every time he does or says something that touches me."

"Vulnerability sucks, doesn't it? We have to put the tender parts of ourselves out there and hope that someone doesn't come along with a chain saw or a grenade or a flamethrower. The sad thing is, if you don't do it, you'll never truly know love. If you don't give your dad the chance to hurt you, then you won't have the closeness you want."

"So...you've never been with a man?"

Alex looked at Dana. "I waxed philosophical there, I think you missed it."

"Oh, I got it. I was hoping you'd come up with an angle that would spare me from having to be human, but nope."

"I'm sorry I'm not more help."

Dana reached over and laid her hand atop Alex's. "Just being with you makes everything better. Life and distance got in the way there for a while. I'm so sorry that I didn't make more of an effort to stay in touch."

Alex stared at the hand atop hers. "I'm equally to blame."

"So it's back to the penis."

Alex's brow shot up. "You want to talk about those?"

Dana turned sideways in her chair and propped her chin in her hand. "I want to talk about you. You said you knew you weren't into guys when you were with Mark. Why didn't you ever tell me that?"

Alex shrugged. "I had to deal with it internally first."

"You could've told me. I could've been your shoulder to lean on, you were always mine. I'm sure you thought I was too young to understand back then, but that's not the case now." Dana narrowed her eyes. "I really sense something is bothering you."

Alex kept her gaze averted but smiled. "I'm fine. You're missing the sunset by staring at me."

"I see it on your face," Dana said as she scooted her chair closer and laid her head on Alex's shoulder. "If we never find the ones we're looking for, let's grow old together. Promise?"

Alex closed her eyes. Dana was killing her. "Promise." She lifted the bottle of wine to her lips and drank.

"What's your type of woman?"

"Trashy, with really big hair and boobs. They wear pants that look like they were poured into them and stripper heels."

Dana laughed. "You ass. Tell me."

"I don't know if I really have a type."

"Can I ask how you met Vanessa?"

"It was a blind date that I really didn't want to go on. My friends Kim and Linda had never met Vanessa. Someone they knew suggested they introduce her to me. I learned later that Vanessa didn't want to go on the date, either, but her friends hounded her until she agreed. I was a total tool and refused to go unless Kim and Linda doubled with us. So we all met at a restaurant, and I felt so sorry for Vanessa because Kim was basically interviewing her. I couldn't get a word in edgewise until Linda very kindly told Kim to shut up. After dinner, Vanessa and I took a walk alone. We realized that we had things in common, and over ice cream, I asked her out again, and she accepted."

"Where'd you take her on your real date?" Dana asked as Alex took a sip of wine.

"We went on a picnic, which reminds me that I brought snacks."

Dana dug into the cooler bag. "What kind of cheesecake is this?"

"One is raspberry and the other is blueberry, I think."

"No, it's chocolate chip," Dana said after she unwrapped one and bit into it. "Oh, now that's good." She held it to Alex's mouth. "Bite." She grinned. "Now that's all you get. You drink the rest of the wine, and I'll take care of this."

"There's no way I can drink a whole bottle by myself."

"I drank the whole thing."

"Yes, you did," Dana said as she half-dragged Alex up the stairs of her house. "You are slap-ass drunk, Alex Soileau."

"I'm really not."

"If I let you go, you'd fall down these stairs. You've forgotten how to use your feet. Step up, silly, and hurry. I hear thunder."

"That's right, we're on the steps," Alex slurred. "There'll be no tossing and turning for me tonight, I'm gonna sleep like…why do people say 'sleep like a log?' That's so stupid, but I was gonna say it."

Dana dragged Alex onto the deck. "Give me your keys."

Alex sighed as she dropped them into Dana's palm. "I doubt I can hit the hole right now anyway. That's really bad for a lesbian to admit."

Dana unlocked the door and pushed it open. "You don't drink very often, do you?"

"Hardly ever. I'm kind of a lightweight when it comes to booze."

Dana wrapped her arm around Alex's waist and led her inside. "You are going to need to drink a lot of water tonight or you're gonna be miserable in the morning. I'll help you get undressed and into bed, then I'll get you something to drink."

Alex pulled away from her and took a few steps on her own. She leaned against the couch and spread her arms out. "I'm fine. I really am. I can get undressed myself."

Dana wasn't so sure. She walked into the kitchen, opened the fridge, and pulled out two bottles of water. "You should drink this now." She handed one to Alex and set another on the coffee table.

Alex opened the lid and drank, spilling some of it down the front of her chin and shirt. "What time do you want to get together tomorrow?"

"How about one, so you can sleep in?" Dana said with a laugh as she wiped Alex's face with her fingers.

Alex nodded. "That works. Should I invite Julia, so Sydney will have someone to hang out with?"

"Sure. Are you gonna be okay?"

Alex grinned. "I'm so fine."

"Right now, you are. I feel kind of guilty for leaving you like this. I want to get you into bed."

"Do you want to know how many women have said that to me?" Alex asked with a snort.

The kicked puppy expression returned to Dana's face as she set her hands on her hips. "Actually, I do."

Alex swayed a little bit. "Oh, damn, you're serious. Do you have a calculator?"

Dana's jaw sagged. "Are *you* serious?"

"No." Alex held up a hand. "This many."

"Okay, five isn't that bad. You had me worried you were a slut."

Alex held her hand up again. "And this many more."

Dana stared at her for a moment brows raised. "Is that hand about to go up again?"

Alex shrugged. "Did I count to ten?"

"You did."

"Then no. I'm done."

Dana stared at her for a moment and wrapped her arms around Alex's shoulders. "I love you, you know that?"

Alex stared at her in a daze. "I love you, too, but you don't know that."

"Yes, I do."

Alex's gaze dropped to Dana's lips, and for a few seconds, Dana thought Alex was going to really kiss her instead of the casual pecks on the cheek that they gave each other. That surprised her less than the realization that she wanted her to. They both seemed to come to their senses at the same time. Alex blinked rapidly as Dana took a step back.

"I'm...I'm gonna go. You lock this door behind me, okay?"

Alex nodded, still looking like she was in a daze.

"Good night." Dana closed the door and listened as Alex locked it. She walked toward the steps and turned when she heard a thud. Through the window, she saw the bottle of water that she'd set on the table rolling around on the floor and Alex sprawled out on the couch.

Chapter 13

Dana drove to the end of Alex's driveway and stopped at the road. She put the car in park and stared at the trees illuminated by her headlights feeling as drunk as Alex was, though she'd only had a few sips of the wine. Most of what Daniel accused Dana of wasn't true, but he had been right about one thing. She didn't like to self-analyze. He'd browbeaten her so much that she had shifted into survival mode. Survivors didn't have time to sit back and contemplate why they did the things they did. Survivors were too busy plotting the next step, and sometimes, that sole focus made them blind to everything else in their lives. Dana had been in the dark for years about herself.

She was contemplating and analyzing now, though. The conversation at sunset had stirred up a volley of emotions and feelings that fluttered in the pit of her stomach. Thunder rumbled and lightning flashed as bits and pieces of things she'd refused to study opened up like a book in her mind. Pictures she couldn't look away from, pictures with very potent feelings attached flashed before her eyes.

Dana could feel a biting cold wind on the back of her neck, as though she were actually in the past watching Alex talk to Mark Lanoux at a school football game. Aimee Perkins and her friends stood nearby, and Dana could hear their conversation.

"They're doing it. Mark said he fucked her like six times."

Dana had turned then and walked home, and told herself

the intense burning in her stomach and chest was anger because Alex was spending time with him and ignoring her. But the adult Dana finally accepted that was not the truth. It wasn't anger that inflamed her, it was jealousy. Lightning flashed again, and another page in her life book seemed to turn.

This time, she felt the sun on her head, the waters of the bay around her. Dana held on to one side of a raft as they floated and Alex held the other. Alex grinned as Dana wrapped her legs around her waist. "Are you gonna try and pull me under?" That had been Dana's original intent, but the warmth of Alex's body between her legs spread out through Dana like a fire. She had no excuse for that sensation; she simply shelved it, refusing to acknowledge what it really was.

Dana put her hands over her face. "Oh, shit."

Dana writhed beneath a warm body, lips upon her neck stoked the fire burning inside of her. She ached for a release that wasn't coming fast enough. Her hands fisted in dark hair. She pulled until her lover's face loomed above her.

"Todd! No, no, no, I don't want this with you. What are you doing here? My dad will tear you limb from limb if he finds you in his house. Are you crazy?"

Todd rolled over and morphed into someone else she didn't recognize, but the need was still urgent inside of Dana as she continued to grind into the stranger who was now beneath her. It felt wrong, intimacy with someone she didn't know, but she couldn't stop. Hands moved over her body; the heat of them drove her mad. Then the face changed, but it was now in shadow. Dana released a sigh of relief when she realized it was Alex. She let herself go and gave into the sensations, but Alex turned away each time she tried to kiss her. *Let me, please, let me.* She heard the words in her mind, but they refused to pass her lips. Then the fire ignited between her legs and fanned out over her body. *Alex, it's you, it's you.*

Dana awoke with a gasp, gripping her pillow, still grinding into the bed. "Oh, shit," she whispered breathlessly and listened as footfalls drew closer to her room. Sydney burst through her door a second later looking horrified.

"Are you okay?"

Dana nodded. "Bad dream...bad, *bad* dream."

Sydney put a hand to her chest and blew out a breath. "You sounded like you were being murdered."

"It was a...bear." Dana pulled her sheet and blanket up to her chin. "I was being mauled."

"I nearly killed myself trying to get out of my bed."

"Sorry...it was a really big bear. Um...are you going to shower?"

"I took one last night, and I saw your note in the bathroom about today. I can't believe we're going skiing," Sydney said excitedly. "Can Julia come with us?"

"Alex said something about inviting her last night, but you may want to call Julia anyway."

"Okay, cool," Sydney said as she sprinted from the room.

Dana put the heel of her hand to her forehead and closed her eyes. At thirty-eight, she'd just had her first wet dream.

Alex reached around, hoping to find her alarm clock and silence it. She was disconcerted that her bed stand was not where she'd last seen it, but her head hurt too much to open her eyes. The really odd thing was it didn't buzz, it sounded like banging.

"Alexandra, are you sick?"

Alex opened one eye and stared up at her mother. "Yes?"

"I knocked and you didn't answer, then I looked in the window and saw you here." Jean put a hand to Alex's forehead. "You don't feel hot, is it a stomach bug? Why didn't you call me?"

"My head hurts."

Jean sniffed. "Your breath smells like Momma's. You're drunk!"

"No...I was...now I'm in pain."

Jean threw her hands on her hips. "You're not a drinker. What got into you?"

"A bottle of wine," Alex said as she winced. "Whisper."

"I won't. If you dance, you've gotta pay the piper. Your daddy sent me over here for his saw. Now get up and find it."

Alex sat up slowly and wiped drool from her cheek. "It's in the hall closet with his extension cord. What time is it?"

"Ten." Jean walked into the kitchen and got a bottle of water out of the fridge. "Honestly, honey, you live like a bachelor in this treehouse. There's no food. I can't even fix you something to eat. Not that I could find anything to cook with." She walked back into the den and handed Alex the water before taking the seat. "Why did you pull a Thelma last night?"

"Dana was driving, so she didn't drink much. We talked for a long time, and I just drank without thinking. The next thing I knew, the bottle was empty."

Jean gazed at Alex sympathetically. "Did she say something to hurt you?"

"No, we had a nice time." Alex pressed the water bottle to her head. Images of the previous evening flitted in and out of her mind, Dana so close, her lips parted. "Did I kiss her?"

"Did you what?"

Alex winced. "I said that out loud, didn't I?"

"Did you kiss her?"

"I...don't think so." Alex sighed. "If I did, Dana will let me know."

"Would she be mad?"

Alex closed her eyes. "No, something far worse. She'll tease me."

"Oh, honey, that's much better than your dearest friend being offended. You are a professional, well-centered woman, start acting like it."

"Yes, ma'am," Alex said, making herself sound like a child.

"Go bathe, then come to the house and eat something. Afterward, I want you to go to the grocery store and buy real food. And for Pete's sake, Alexandra, do something with what can only be loosely described as a kitchen."

"I'll start tomorrow."

"Save your gas, we'll take my car," Dana said as she watched Sydney stuff her things into a backpack. "I'll meet you in the kitchen."

Dana walked down the stairs feeling like she was the one with the hangover. She wanted to see Alex, and at the same time, she didn't. Alex was the person she knew she could go to with her problems, but the problem was, Alex was the problem.

"Hi, Dad, anything exciting?" she asked as she walked into the kitchen.

Daniel gazed up at her from the paper. "Big sale at Truss bait and tackle. The Maggios bought an emu and another llama. Wow," he deadpanned.

"I made some sandwiches for your day." Clara set a small cooler on the counter with a broad smile. "Alex loves my walnut chicken salad. Go into the pantry, there's some single-serving bags of chips in there."

"You spoil me, Clara."

"I noticed that you had to stretch out the hose to water the garden. Would you like me to have the service install a sprinkler system?" Daniel asked.

"Oh, Dad, don't go to that expense or trouble. It isn't going to hurt me to put in a little effort." Dana pulled out a few bags of chips and set them on the counter. Then she walked over to where Daniel sat. "What're you going to do today?"

"Clara is going to load me into that land barge she calls a car and take me over to Nate's. He's building a cabinet, and I'm going to supervise, though I have no clue how to do something like that, while Clara visits with her grandchildren."

"I can take you," Dana offered.

Clara was steadily adding bags of chips to Dana's pile and said, "Oh, no, dear, I'll take him. Your father gives me a good excuse to leave when he gets ready for a nap, besides James lives just down the street from Nate."

"Give my regards to Alex when you see her and invite her back to dinner," Daniel said with a smile as he watched Sydney bound into the kitchen.

"I will." Dana watched as Sydney walked over and kissed Daniel on the cheek. She swallowed hard and followed suit. Daniel's eyes widened for a second, then he graced her with a bright smile.

"We'll see y'all later, and, Clara, thank you again for all the trouble."

"None at all, dear."

Sydney carried the cooler and the bag that Clara handed her out to the car and put them in the backseat. "Mom, there's an ice chest already back here, and there's what looks like a festering piece of cake and cheese in it."

"Oh, I forgot to take that inside last night. Empty that in the trash, please."

Dana settled in the driver's seat and started the car. Sydney joined her a minute later with a grin. "There was a cork in there, too. You had a picnic last night?"

Dana looked away. "No, Alex and I went to watch the sunset with snacks."

"Uh-huh," Sydney said as she stared out the passenger's window.

"What does that mean?"

"It's a commonly used acknowledgment. Was the sunset pretty?"

Dana glanced at Sydney as she pulled out of the driveway. "What's so funny?"

"The bear that you dreamed about, was it named...Alex? Because that's what you were calling it."

Dana's face grew hot. "I did not. That's not what you said this morning."

"Because I was too embarrassed." Sydney's body shook with laughter. "You sounded like you were having sex, but when you screamed, it scared me. That must've been some mauling."

"It was a mauling, and Alex was getting it, too…the bear was getting her, too. Let's drop it."

Sydney sank down in the seat holding her stomach as she laughed.

"If you say anything to—"

"Oh, my God, I couldn't. There's no way."

"No jokes."

Sydney wiped her eyes and tried to recover, but she started laughing again.

Dana pursed her lips. "It *was* a bear."

They picked Julia up first and headed over to Alex's place. Dana watched as she came down the stairs in a pair of red board shorts and a white- and red-striped bikini top. A red ball cap was on her head backward. The butterflies that had been in Dana's stomach the night before awakened and began to flutter as Alex walked over to her window.

"The boat is at the neighbor's dock. It's within walking distance."

Dana was so taken aback by the feelings swirling around inside of her that her foot slipped from the brake and the car began to move before she even noticed. She reacted by slamming on it.

"Mom, oh, my God." Sydney stared at her like she was insane.

Dana threw up her hands. "Flip-flop malfunction. I'm sorry." She smiled up at Alex sheepishly. "I'll just park here."

Alex grinned at Julia and Sydney when they got out of the car. "Are y'all ready to do some skiing?"

"I'm totally pumped," Sydney said.

"And I'm going to remember to let go of the rope this time when I fall. Oh! I wore shorts that have a drawstring, so I won't lose my bottoms." Julia looked at Sydney. "I mooned a bunch of people the last time. It really wasn't pretty."

Dana climbed out of the car and tried to play it cool. "Clara sends her regards and walnut chicken salad sandwiches."

Alex clenched her fists and looked up to the sky. "I love that woman!"

"You look surprisingly well today," Dana said softly and pulled the cooler from the backseat.

"I took some pain relievers, drank like a gallon of water, then I went by the office and breathed in some oxygen, which really helped with the headache. Before that, I was pretty pathetic." Alex watched as the girls walked over to the wishing well and lowered her voice. "Did I do anything embarrassing or something I should apologize for?"

Dana smiled. "You made me drag your ass up those stairs, but other than that, you were well behaved."

"Okay, good to know," Alex said with a sigh of relief. "Are you going to ski?"

"Um, no. I'll leave that to the kids. I really don't want to moon anyone."

Alex took the cooler from Dana. "There's a trail over here."

"We're leaving," Dana called to the kids as she followed Alex.

Seconds later, Julia and Sydney raced past them.

"You really made Sydney's day by inviting us out on your boat. She loves the water," Dana said.

"That makes me happy. It's something I enjoy, too." Alex glanced at Dana. "She's a cool kid, so is Julia. We'll have a good time dragging them around the bay."

Sydney and Julia were already in the boat when Dana and Alex made it to the dock. Alex handed the cooler to Julia and climbed in. She smiled as she held out her hand. Dana took it and noticed the smirk on Sydney's face as Alex helped her into the boat. Dana thumped Sydney on the ear as she walked by.

Dana watched Alex as she untied and threw off the lines. The low-slung shorts showed off a flat belly and narrow hips.

It was early spring, but Alex's skin was already golden brown. "You always did tan so easily, you make me sick with jealousy," Dana said as Alex moved past her and sat at the helm.

"I've got the Soileau skin like my daddy. Andrew and Malcolm were always so jealous because, as you know, they got Mom's fair skin. Speaking of fair, I have sunscreen if you haven't already put some on."

"I did," Dana said with a nod. "I coated myself in it before I got dressed. Sydney, did you screen up?"

"Yep, I'm greasy as a pig."

Dana smiled at Julia. "How about you, sweetie?"

"I practically took a bath in it. I got blistered the last time I came out on the boat," Julia said with a pained expression. "I had on sunscreen, but I missed the bottom of my butt cheeks. I couldn't sit down for like a week." She grinned. "I had a real case of the red ass."

Alex backed away from the dock and slowly moved out toward open water. She glanced at Dana, who was still staring at her. "Is something wrong?"

Dana was mortified that she'd been caught and put on her sunglasses. "You're so…brown…like a dinner roll. You know how they're so white when they go in the oven, then they get… golden?"

Sydney snorted with laughter, but the outburst was drowned by the sound of the motor as Alex gunned it and took off. They rode for a few minutes, and Alex slowed and killed the engine. "Dana, I elect you to be watch while I drive. If they go down or signal for me to stop, I'll rely on you to tell me. Who wants to go first, or are y'all going together?"

Julia turned to Sydney. "If you want to try to slalom, you should do it while your legs are still strong, so I'm good if you wanna go first."

"You really don't mind?" Sydney asked excitedly.

Julia shook her head. "I ski all the time with my dad."

"Okay!" Sydney stood and prepared to jump into the water before Alex caught her.

"Hold on a minute, sparky, you have to have a vest on." She pulled one out of a storage compartment and held it up to Sydney. "This will fit."

Sydney shrugged into it and tightened the straps around her waist and chest, but Alex gave them a final yank to make sure they were tight. Julia attached the rope to the back of the boat and tossed the slalom ski into the water.

Alex tapped Sydney on the shoulder. "Thumbs-up means you're good to go, thumbs-down means you want me to stop or wait while you get adjusted. I'm sure you know to lean back, keep the tip of your ski out of the water, and keep your body taut."

Sydney nodded. "Like regular skiing, my weight is just positioned on one ski."

"I put more pressure down with my right foot when I'm coming up," Julia offered. "You just gotta do your own thing until you get it right."

Alex laughed as she shoved Sydney out of the boat, but when she turned around, she noticed that Dana wasn't laughing, too. "Was I being too rough?"

"Hmm…oh, no, I was just daydreaming."

"Is something bothering you?" Alex asked as she climbed back into her seat and started the motor.

This was the perfect setup for Dana to reply, *I think I may be in love with you, probably have been for most of my life, but I've been in denial, so please excuse me while I have the mother of all fucking epiphanies.* Instead, she said, "No, I'm good."

"Ready?" Julia called out, and Sydney raised her thumb.

Alex moved slowly for a moment to take the slack out of the rope, then took off. For a second, Sydney came up out of the water. Dana smiled. "She's up, she's doing…she's down."

After about twenty "she's downs," Sydney finally got up. She rode in the wake behind the boat for a while before she grew confident enough to cross to the smooth water. The transition was awkward, but Sydney managed to stay upright.

Alex glanced over her shoulder often. "She's doing good."

"Yeah, I'm proud of her," Dana said with a smile.

"Sure you don't want to give it a whirl? I know you can do it, we used to go all the time."

Dana shook her head. "Not today."

"She's down," Julia announced with a laugh.

Something was up with Dana, and it was beginning to make Alex nervous. Her brain had been pickled the night before, but she was aware of the mistake she'd almost made. She just wasn't sure if she'd done a good job of covering it up. Dana didn't seem angry or put off when she'd said good night, but something was obviously under her skin.

When Sydney tired, Julia went out. She sprang out of the water like a champ and got some pretty decent height when she jumped the wake. Sydney pounded her thighs. "Man! I want to be able to do that."

"By midsummer, you will," Alex said with a smile. "It just takes practice, and we'll come out as often as your schedule allows."

"Sweet! Thanks."

Alex glanced over her shoulder and looked at Julia, then at Sydney. "Do you like Barbier Point?"

"I thought it was gonna suck, but it's not too bad. The people I work with are all right. Julia's cool, but she's going to LSU in the fall, which stinks because I'm not gonna know anyone when I go back to school."

"You should call her the next time you're off work. She's got a lot of friends, and she'd be more than happy to introduce you to them," Alex said.

"We already talked about it. I'm off Wednesday because I have to work all next weekend. Julia and I are gonna go out Tuesday night. Somebody she knows is having a fish fry."

Dana watched Julia as she was coming back over the wake. Somehow, she hit it wrong and did a complete flip. The ski shot off like a rocket as Julia seemed to skid across the surface of the water on her shoulders, legs flailing in the air.

Always Alex

"She's down!" Dana said as Alex slowed and turned. "That was a bad wipeout. She went down on her head, I hope she didn't hurt her neck."

Julia bobbed in the water facing away from them, and for a moment, she didn't respond to their shouts. As Alex drew close, Julia finally seemed to get her senses back. She sputtered and coughed for a moment.

"Whoa! Did anyone video that?" Julia asked, eyes wide.

Sydney shook her head. "No, I was running my mouth. Are you okay?"

"I'm fine. That was totally awesome, but the ride ripped my boobs out of my suit. I gotta put 'em back in." Julia turned her back and reached inside the vest. "Ew, I drank some bay, too."

"Get up here and let me have a look at you." Alex held out a hand and hoisted Julia up. "How's your neck?"

"Doesn't hurt at all. Nothing hurts but my ears, and my sinuses are filled with water." Julia smacked her lips. "I hate it when I swallow that nasty crap."

Alex got a bottle of water out of the cooler and handed it to her. "You take a break for a little while."

After they retrieved the ski, Alex let the boat drift and they had lunch. Dana watched as Alex virtually inhaled one sandwich and opened another. "Were you hungry?"

Alex rolled her eyes as she chewed and swallowed. "I love Clara's chicken salad. She always brings me sandwiches when your dad has an appointment. The way she cuts them into little triangles and trims off the crust just spells love to me," she said in a goofy voice.

Julia shielded her eyes against the sun and said, "I think that's Debbie Langlois headed this way."

Alex turned and watched as a boat approached them. "Yep, that's her." She turned to Dana. "Debbie and Kendra are one of the lesbian couples that live in town. They're nice people. I think you'll like them."

The boat slowed and coasted near them. "Hey, Alex, you got trouble?" the woman behind the wheel asked.

Alex held up her sandwich. "Lunch break. Let me introduce you to one of my oldest and dearest friends and her daughter." Alex put a hand on Dana's shoulder. "This is Dana Castilaw and her daughter, Sydney. Of course, you know Julia." Alex waved a hand at her friends. "This is Debbie Langlois and Kendra Wieland, and I don't believe I've met your passenger, Deb."

"This is Judy Owen, she's from Houma, and we finally talked her into coming out on the water with us." Deb shot Alex an odd little smile. "I'd hoped we might run into you."

Everyone exchanged hellos and a "nice to meet you." The couple with the matching spiky haircuts seemed nice to Dana, but when it came to Judy, her hackles rose. She was pretty, blond, with a flawless figure, and her green gaze roved over Alex with appreciation. Dana felt she knew the meaning of Deb's smile; she wanted Judy and Alex to meet. Dana watched Alex closely behind her dark glasses for any show of interest in Judy. Every time Judy smiled at Alex, something inside of Dana smoldered. She tried to maintain a pleasant expression, though she was tempted to scowl at Judy and fantasized about shoving her overboard. Her hand shook slightly as she rubbed her forehead.

Sydney leaned over and put a hand on Dana's thigh. "You okay?" she asked with concern.

"Uh-huh, yeah." Dana forced a smile. "I had too much coffee for breakfast, I have the jitters."

Sydney pulled another sandwich from the cooler and handed it to Dana. "You should eat."

"Thank you, baby."

Dana nibbled at the sandwich, overwhelmed with feelings. She'd analyzed herself so much she felt like a computer being defragmented. She needed to talk to someone, wanted someone to help her make sense of everything she thought she was feeling, but there was no one but Alex who she trusted enough to purge her soul to. So Dana tried to manufacture the conversation in her mind.

Okay, here's my problem, Alex. I've always loved you, and as I look back on my life, I think I may've always been in love with you. I can admit now that I was jealous of Mark. I'm jealous of Collette now. I'm about to shove that Judy bitch off the boat. And you make me horny just looking at you. I've found women sexually attractive, and well, look at my track record. I really don't have a whole lot of interest in men. Yes, I know I married one, but what attracted me to him was his resemblance to you. At this point, I'm pretty sure I'm gay. This is not the problem. I just don't know if any of this is real or if I'm just losing my damn mind. Can I touch your—

"Mom?"

"Yes?"

Sydney pointed at the sandwich Dana was holding. She'd squeezed it in half, and the chicken salad inside was lying on the bottom of the boat.

"I'm gonna call you this week, maybe we can get together Wednesday or Thursday night," Deb said and looked at Judy. "You're not on shift then, are you?"

"No, I'm free," Judy said and smiled at Alex.

Debbie turned the engine on her boat. "Hey, it was really nice meeting ya'll."

"Nice to meet y'all, too," Dana said with a little wave, but she really wanted to shoot them the finger. She looked at her hand wondering if she actually had.

Chapter 14

"Are they ready?"

"Yep, both thumbs up." Dana held on when Alex took off, pulling Julia and Sydney out of the water.

Alex glanced over her shoulder occasionally and let her gaze track over Dana as she faced forward. Dana had become even more withdrawn since they stopped for lunch. Alex couldn't see her eyes behind the glasses she wore, but when Dana was in thought about something, she chewed her bottom lip, and she had been steadily chomping on it for almost an hour.

"What's troubling you?"

Dana's brows shot up over the top of her glasses as she turned to Alex. "Nothing. Why?"

"You can't lie to me. I know you better than I know myself."

"Oh…I don't think you do. There are some days I don't even know me. Are you gonna go out with that floozy-looking woman?"

Alex glanced at her. "What woman?"

"Judy. It was pretty obvious that Deb intends to hook you two up."

"What's wrong with her?"

"She flipped her hair too much, and she leered at you. She's too pretty, and those kinds of women are nothing but trouble. Her boobs were fake, too. Nobody with that little body fat has a rack like that, and natural breasts don't sit that high. Those things were poking out of her collarbones." Dana shook her head. "Not a good choice for you."

"I'm getting the impression you didn't like her."

Dana shrugged. "I don't think she's worthy of you."

Alex stared at Dana's profile for a second. "Okay, noted."

"Good."

When dark clouds began to gather on the horizon, Alex headed for shore before the water got rough. She wanted another opportunity to talk to Dana alone, but as soon as the boat was cleaned out, Dana was headed for her car. Sydney seemed just as confused by the abrupt departure as Alex did.

"Are y'all fighting?" she asked in a whisper as she walked alongside Alex on the trail.

"I don't think so, but she seems really pissed off. Did she have an argument with your grandpa before y'all came over here?"

"No, she even kissed him goodbye when we left, and I haven't seen them do that before."

Alex sighed and tried to smile. "She's probably just tired. We did stay out kind of late last night."

"She had a bad dream, too, something about a bear. She woke up screaming." Sydney cleared her throat. "Yeah, she's probably tired."

By the time they got to the car, Dana and Julia were already inside. Dana rolled down her window with her sunglasses still on, even though the skies had turned dark with storm clouds, and smiled apologetically. "I'm sorry to rush off, but I've got a bad headache."

"That's okay. Do you want to take something for it now? You might feel better by the time you get home. I have some pain relievers upstairs."

"No, but thanks. I'll call you, okay?"

Alex stepped away from the car as Dana began to back up and watched as she drove away. "Okay."

§

Sydney smiled and waved at Julia. "See you Tuesday." As soon as she rolled up the window, she turned to Dana. "What on earth is wrong with you?"

"Headache. You didn't ask me if you could go out on Tuesday night."

"Julia and I only just talked about it today when we were over by the well. Can I go?"

"Yes."

Sydney wrapped her towel tighter around herself and turned the AC down a notch. "Did I do something to make you mad?"

"No, baby."

"Did Alex?"

"No."

"Then why do you look that way?"

"I told you, I have a headache."

"But you look mad."

Dana ripped her sunglasses off and threw them on the dashboard. "I'm not mad, okay?"

"Okay." Sydney turned and looked out the window.

They made the ride home in silence. When they got to the house, Dana went straight upstairs and took a shower. Then she went into her room and closed the door. After Sydney showered, she decided to go downstairs for a snack, but when she passed Dana's door, she thought she heard her crying. Without bothering to knock, she went in and found Dana curled up on her bed. Sydney closed the door and walked over to her.

"Mom, tell me what's going on," Sydney said worriedly as she laid a hand on Dana's shoulder. "Are you sick? Should I get Grandpa?"

"No." Dana sat up and wiped her eyes. "I'm okay."

Sydney sat on the bed. "No, you're not, you never cry.

Okay, I saw you do it once when you hit your finger with a hammer. You're kinda freaking me out. Do you want me to get Clara instead?"

Dana shook her head. "No, honey, everything's okay. I'm just dealing with some things right now..." Dana waved a hand. "...that I don't know how to deal with."

"Then tell me about it. I'm not a little girl anymore, I'm almost eighteen."

Dana pulled her knees up and set her chin on them as she debated opening up to Sydney. They talked about pretty much everything else, but she wasn't sure how Sydney would react. Then she was reminded of the speech she'd given to Sydney about talking to her and felt hypocritical.

"I'm just gonna put it out there."

Sydney moved up farther on the bed. "Okay."

"I'm just gonna say it, and it may sound crazy."

Sydney nodded. "I'm ready."

"I'm just gonna say—"

"Mom."

"I...think I'm gay." When Sydney didn't react, Dana said, "I'm not joking."

"I didn't think you were."

"Then why don't you look surprised?"

Sydney scrunched up her face. "I'm not being disrespectful, but, Mom, you're kinda...slow."

Dana's brows rose. "Why do you say that?"

"You've been divorced since I was three. You've only gone out a handful of times with a few guys. You wear Tevas, you drive a Subaru, you have every Melissa Etheridge CD ever made, and your favorite color is purple."

Dana shrugged. "What does purple have to do with anything?"

"I don't know, I was on a roll and just threw that in. Honestly, all those things don't make me think you're gay, it's the way you look at Alex. Julia noticed, too. She asked me if y'all were dating. I think it's time you admit that it's a lot more than just a galmance." Sydney put a hand on Dana's shoulder. "Why are you crying again?"

"She had a boyfriend in school named Mark, and I hated him. He used to leave the windows of his Camaro down a little bit in the summer, and one day, I stuffed rotten shrimp inside of it. The whole time I was scrubbing my hands with lemons to get the smell out, I told myself I did it because she was too good for him." Dana sniffed. "I figured that if his car stunk, she wouldn't ride with him anymore."

Sydney smiled. "That's gross, but—"

"And there was this girl who always wanted to hang out with us, but I didn't want her to because she was Alex's age and I was afraid Alex would start to like her more. So I poured soda into Alex's favorite school bag. It was really cool, only the track team had them." Dana's face contorted. "I told Alex that Sandy did it, and she believed me because I was her best friend." She sobbed.

"Okay, I know we're not practicing Catholics, but maybe you need to go to confession and…a psychiatrist."

Dana wiped her face and sniffed. "I did these things when I was a kid never understanding why. Later on, I did think about it a little and figured that I was just threatened by anyone who would take her away from me. But I realized last night that no one has ever made me feel the way she does. I think I've been trying to replace her all these years and I never could. Now that we're back here and I'm around her, I just feel…happy, kind of complete, like I've found what I lost."

Sydney traced the pattern on Dana's comforter with her finger. "Are you sexually—"

"Trust me when I say, yeah, very…yeah. Let's not go down that road." Dana sniffed and cleared her throat. "Are you?"

"Turned on by Alex? No," Sydney said with a laugh, then sobered when she met Dana's eye. "That's how I figured you out so easily. It kind of takes one to know one…you know? I knew you were on to me, too. You asked a lot of questions about Leighton."

"Then why didn't you tell me?"

Sydney looked away. "Because I knew you'd have a problem with her spending the night all the time."

Dana closed her eyes. "You slept with her."

"I love her," Sydney said softly. "Her dad's a liar. He's not going to let her come here for a visit. She asked him about it again, and he told her he changed his mind." Her gaze slowly rose to meet Dana's. "But the second she graduates, she's coming here. That's the real reason I'm working so many hours. I do want to help you with the bills, but I'm saving up so when she gets here, we can eventually get a place together."

"Oh, Sydney," Dana said with a sigh. "What about college, baby?"

"I'm still going, and Leighton wants to be a radiology technician. Her aunt is a nurse, and she's going to help her apply for those schools." Sydney held Dana's gaze for a minute. "Her aunt said I could stay with them, too. She knows about me and Leighton. Besides, I can't live here and drive back and forth to school in New Orleans every day."

"I thought...I figured we'd be back in New Orleans by then."

"What about Alex?"

Dana released a shuddering breath. "I don't know."

"You're not gonna tell her how you feel?"

"Oh, I'm not sure what she's going to think about that. I know her so well, but this part I don't." Dana threw her hands up in the air. "Hey, Alex, guess what? I'm gay, too, and I think I'm in love with you. How about that?"

Sydney laughed. "Again, not being disrespectful, but you really are slow...or blind. She looks at you the same way you do her. You should probably tell her how you feel because I'd bet you my phone that she's gonna say the same thing."

"Your phone? That's big," she said with a laugh. "So... how long have you been involved with Leighton?"

"Since eighth grade." Sydney held up a hand when Dana's jaw dropped. "We didn't do...anything until..." She cleared her throat. "...we were...older."

Dana gestured for a second as she tried to reconcile that Sydney had obviously been sexually active for a while. "How did this come about?"

"She used to tell me that I was cute all the time," Sydney said with a wistful smile. "I've always thought she was beautiful. I was going kinda crazy because I had feelings for her, and I was afraid that she'd be freaked out. But at the same time, I felt she liked me that way, too, because she was always touching me, and she held my hand a lot. Then one day, she just kissed me, and I knew everything was gonna be okay. I told her everything, and she admitted that she'd had a crush on me since the sixth grade."

"Have your feelings for her changed at all since you've been apart?"

Sydney nodded. "They grow stronger. She says she feels the same. We talk every night until we fall asleep."

Dana blew out a breath and smiled. "Thank God for unlimited calling plans."

Sydney was serious when she said, "I'm always going to love her. Her aunt says we're young and things change when you live with one another, that's why she wants us to stay with her. That kind of makes me mad because it's like she's saying that what we have isn't real."

Dana chewed her bottom lip. "That is true. You really learn about a person when you have to depend on them. Sometimes, you let each other down, but how you work that out determines whether or not the relationship will work." Dana smiled. "I don't think age has as much to do with that as people think."

"I'm gonna marry Leighton one day," Sydney said with resolve, then grinned. "Maybe we can have a double wedding with you and Alex."

Dana laughed. "Well, I have to get the girl first."

"Slo-mo, you've already got her."

Chapter 15

Alex grunted as she hefted one of the kitchen cabinets over the railing of her deck and listened with satisfaction as it landed on the others that she'd already pitched out. After Dana left, Alex got a pry bar and a hammer and started ripping the kitchen apart. She needed something to do to quell the mounting fear that Dana had figured her out and was upset. She walked back inside, put her hands on her hips, and stared at her gutted kitchen as sweat poured down her face. The only thing left to do was to rip out the linoleum tiles.

She picked up a scraper and was about to get to work when she heard her cellphone chime, indicating she had a text message. Alex picked it up and read: *Meet me under the tree in an hour?*

Alex swallowed hard and replied: *Yes*. She dropped the tool on the floor and headed for the shower.

Alex's hands shook as she held the steering wheel. As she bathed, she tried to think of all the things Dana might say and hoped her assumptions were wrong. But the closer she got to Dana's house, the more she worried that Dana would utter the words Alex never wanted to hear—I could never love you like that.

Alex drove past the house to where the road ended at the marsh and parked like she always had when they were younger. She pulled a bottle of water from the drink holder and drank, wishing she had some of Thelma's Mad Dog to calm her nerves. She was pretty certain that after that night she would be sitting on the porch with Maw Maw drinking away her blues and singing *Silver Wangs*.

Under the tree, Dana was having heart palpitations. She'd seen Alex's car pass and knew she would be here soon. If Sydney was wrong in believing that Alex felt the same, Dana was so screwed. Alex would be kind and let her down gently, then Dana was pretty certain that she would lock herself in her room and cry until Monday morning when she had to go to work.

She plastered herself against the tree and hid in the shadows as she spotted Alex walking across the lawn. "Oh, my God, oh, my God, what am I doing?" Dana whispered as she clawed at the bark. The closer Alex got, the louder Dana's pulse pounded in her ears. She felt like everyone in Barbier Point could hear it.

Alex walked beneath the shadows of the boughs and stared up at the house. It took Dana a minute to whisper, "I'm over here."

"Hey," Alex said as she drew closer. "What's up?"

"Well…it's funny. I've been doing a lot of thinking, and… you smell good."

"Thanks, I bathed." Alex tried to stuff her hands into the pockets of her running shorts and realized she didn't have any. She folded her arms instead. "What were you thinking about?"

Dana licked her lips. "Do you remember someone putting shrimp in Mark's car?"

"Yeah, that was foul."

"I did it."

Alex laughed softly. "Why?"

"I hated him."

"I did too sometimes."

"Sandy didn't pour Orange Crush in your track bag…I did that, too."

Alex's arms dropped to her sides. "Do you know how much I loved that bag? It had a really cool bobcat on it. Nobody had them but the track team."

"I know, and I'm sorry," Dana said, thankful that Alex's face was in shadow and she was hidden, too. "I was jealous of Sandy and Mark."

"You didn't have to be. You knew you were my very best friend, no one would've ever taken your place. No one ever has. I still have that bag, by the way. It took me forever to get the sticky out, but the bobcat is still orange."

"So I've been thinking a lot—"

"Wait, the shrimp and the soda weren't what you were thinking about?" Alex asked, disappointed that wasn't what Dana wanted to discuss.

"No." Dana exhaled loudly. "So I've been thinking a lot about myself. Have you ever felt like you kind of thought you had yourself figured out, but then you realized that you really didn't? And suddenly, some things made sense but others like totally freaked you out and you were like, man, where did that come from? But it was really right, and in your gut, you just knew it was the truth?"

"Kinda...huh?"

"Alex...I'm..." Dana swallowed hard. "I'm...well... I'm...in...love with you."

That was not what Alex expected to hear. "What?"

Dana slapped the tree. "Sydney!"

Alex strained her eyes in the darkness. "Is she out here, too?"

"No!"

What Dana had said finally registered in Alex's brain, and her knees went weak. She sat down, and the wet grass from the earlier storm soaked through her shorts unnoticed. "You're in love with me?" she asked, her voice full of wonder.

Dana turned around and hugged the tree for support. She leaned her head against the cool bark and closed her eyes. "That's what I was trying to explain a minute ago. I was never sexually attracted to Troy, and I had this kind of encounter with a woman one night in a bar. It wasn't sex, but it turned me on, and that's what I thought about when I had sex with him. I kind of figured that I was gay, but back then, Sydney was so little, and I was afraid of trying to raise her alone... I tried to date other guys that I thought would make good fathers, but when they made advances, I dumped them. Then one day, I realized that I was taking care of Sydney on my own just fine, so I didn't date anymore. But I worked my ass off, and there was no time to think about what I wanted. Then I lost my job, and I came here. When I saw you again, everything was right with the world. I was stressed about living with Dad, the new job is scary, but when I'm with you, everything feels perfect."

Dana hugged the tree a little tighter. She knew she was talking too much and probably not making sense, but she couldn't stop. "When you left for school, my world was empty. I had it in my head that I needed to be married, needed someone to take care of me, so I found someone. Life was empty then, too, except for Sydney. I didn't know it. I didn't know that I had fallen for you, and I looked for someone to fill that space. I never found them. It was always you, and I know that now. I've been in love with you all this time."

"I've loved you, too. I think I started falling when I was eleven and we used to play settlers. I...wished for you on every coin I tossed into the well. That's why I couldn't tell you my wish." Alex felt like she was going to pass out. "I can't get up."

"Well, I can't walk over there because the tree is the only thing keeping me upright at the moment."

"This is why you acted the way you did today. I thought you had figured out how I felt, and it made you uncomfortable. Now I understand why you didn't like Judy."

"Yeah, you thought I was jealous back then? Whew, girl, it's a whole new ballgame."

Alex blew out a breath and stood. She stared at Dana for a second. "You really are hugging that tree."

"Yes, I am."

Alex walked over to her. "Would you mind hugging me instead?"

"I'm real nervous," Dana said as she released it slowly, then reached for Alex.

"Tell me this isn't a dream," Alex said with a sigh as she held Dana closely.

"It's not." Dana sniffed the skin of Alex's neck. "You smell so good, you always did."

Alex put her finger beneath Dana's chin and lifted her face. Dana's lips were so soft, so sweet. No kiss had ever meant as much. Alex moaned as it deepened.

To Dana, it was like pure velvet. She felt like she was melting as one kiss blended into another. They were perfect kisses; they felt like she'd always heard a kiss was supposed to be. They made her heart pound, her knees weak, made her want more of anything Alex had to offer.

Alex pulled her mouth away with a gasp and held Dana tight. "I swear to you that I have never been happier in my life than this moment. I love you. I love this tree. I love the mud soaking my butt. I love you."

Dana laughed softly. "Apparently, I've waited a lifetime to hear those words. I love you, too. Were you going to kiss me last night?"

"You did notice. I was so close, then I caught myself."

"I wanted you to, and it shocked me. That's what really brought everything into perspective. I sat at the end of your driveway thinking. I was a basket case by this evening because I was trying to sort it all out, and Sydney was surprisingly the one I talked to. She said I was slow and that she already figured us out. She's also a lesbian."

"I definitely got that vibe from her."

"She's in love with Leighton, and she's waiting for her to finish school, so she can come here. It's sweet, but had she told me that before I came to my senses, I would've discounted it as puppy love. But it happened to me too a long time ago. I fell in love, and it's lasted all this time."

"For both of us," Alex said as she placed tender kisses on Dana's forehead.

Dana nuzzled her neck. "I'd like to spend Memorial Day with you tomorrow."

"You can have all of my tomorrows," Alex promised with a kiss.

"And you can have mine." She laid her head on Alex's shoulder. "We are so corny now, but I like it."

Chapter 16

Alex jumped out of bed the next morning and raced into her bathroom. She clenched her fists and grinned. "It wasn't a dream," she said as she stared at her shorts with the muddy butt lying on the floor.

At the Castilaw house, Dana awoke and rolled over quickly to look at the shirt she'd been wearing the night before. It hung on a chair where Dana left it to dry. Evidence of the encounter with Alex was displayed in muddy handprints on the sleeves and back of the shirt. "It wasn't a dream," Dana said with a sigh. She bolted out of bed, ran down the hall to Sydney's room, and launched herself on the bed.

Sydney groaned at being pounced on and the stinky breath kisses showering her face. "Mom, I gotta pee, get off."

"She loves me. You were right. All the wishes she made at the well were for me."

Sydney stared into the excited face inches from her own. "Your breath smells like ass."

Dana grinned. "Yours does, too. Did you hear me? She loves me."

Sydney smiled. "I heard. Momma's got a girlfriend, Momma's got a girlfriend," she sang.

Dana put a hand over Sydney's mouth. "You can't tell anyone. I want some time with her before I tell Dad. I want to bask in the bliss for a little while."

"You mean you want to get laid," Sydney said when Dana released her mouth.

"Okay, that part is not something I want to discuss with you."

"And I'm totally good with not hearing it. Are you going to see her today?"

Dana nodded. "I'm about to take a shower, then I'm going over there."

"Remember to shave."

Dana gave Sydney's face a little squeeze. "You're so cute. I'm going to ignore all of your crass comments. I love you."

"Love you, too." Sydney laughed as Dana jumped up and skipped across the room. "Be safe, wear gloves."

Dana went into the bathroom, put a fresh blade in her razor, and stepped into the shower. Excitement, arousal, and nervous anticipation all swirled in the pit of her stomach like a tornado. She wanted Alex, desired to explore every inch of her body, and shower it with affection. Physical intimacy, sex, Dana had no problem with; getting it right, pleasing Alex made her nervous. She knew Alex and was aware that Alex would be extremely patient with her. What made Dana's knees knock was revealing that part of herself to Alex. Being naked was a problem.

Alex's body had never known the trauma of pregnancy and childbirth. Dana ran a hand over her stomach and sighed, thinking it looked like a can of biscuits had exploded. There were a lot of windows in Alex's bedroom, letting in a lot of light. "I wonder if she'd let me blindfold her."

"This is a problem." Alex dropped bags of groceries on her couch. The refrigerator was in the living room. Her microwave sat on a table made of sawhorses next to the coffeemaker.

She had bought fruit, cookies, crackers, cheeses, sports drinks, a bottle of wine, bread, and a frozen lasagna. Most of it went into the fridge, but she ended up stacking the rest on the table and on top of the microwave. She couldn't cook Dana a romantic meal.

This was very important to Alex because she wanted to show Dana that she could take care of her. She wanted Dana to feel like the house was a home, but at the moment, to Alex, it did feel like a treehouse as her mother described it. She knew she was making long-term plans, and she and Dana hadn't even discussed what the revelation of their feelings meant.

When Alex heard a car door slam, she ran onto the deck and watched with a smile as Dana climbed the stairs. She held her arms out, and Dana rushed into them. "I missed you," Alex said as she showered Dana's mouth and face with kisses.

Dana smiled at her. "I feel kind of like I'm seeing you for the very first time. I know every part of you, but being the recipient of your affection is new."

Alex took Dana's hand and led her inside. "I was always careful not to be too touchy with you. I wanted to, but when we were kids, I felt like it was wrong because you were younger. As an adult, I was afraid that you'd realize that I was in love with you and be repelled."

"I'm anything but," Dana said as her gaze swept over Alex.

But she missed the smoldering look as she waved a hand at the kitchen. "This is bad, I know. You must think I'm content to live like a Neanderthal with a cool bathroom. To be honest, I haven't been too enthused about working on the house, but I am now." Alex turned and gazed at Dana. "I want you to help me pick out what goes back into the kitchen."

Dana glanced at the windows. "I noticed that you don't have any blinds or curtains in here. Do you have them in your bedroom?"

"Blinds, but no curtains. That's something else I really need to—"

"Are they room-darkening blinds?"

Alex shook her head. "Not really. I should put some curtains in there because in the morning—"

"Hang blankets over them."

"That's so trashy," Alex said. "I will get curtains, but blinds in here are the priority."

Dana grabbed her face. "Okay, sweetie, you're missing my cues. I'm bashful, I don't want to feel like I'm naked under a spotlight."

Alex's eyes grew wide. "Oh." She swallowed. "I've got lots of blankets."

Dana's nerves began to get the best of her. "I'm not saying we have to go in there right now, but who are we kidding? We're going to end up in there eventually, and I really need it to be kind of dark."

Alex's eyes glazed over. "I'm so incredibly turned on by what you just said, but now my legs feel like jelly."

Dana smiled. "We've been through so much together, we should be able to handle this, too."

"I'm gonna go…get some blankets."

"And I'll help." Dana followed Alex down the hall.

In the closet, Alex handed Dana an armload of the heaviest blankets she had. Then she pulled out a ladder. In the kitchen, she retrieved a hammer and a box of nails.

Dana looked stunned as Alex climbed up the ladder with the corner of a blanket in her hand and a nail in her mouth. "You aren't seriously going to make a hole in the wall with that, are you?"

"Oh, yeah, hand me the hammer. Curtain rods will cover the spots anyway, and if they don't, I know how to drywall."

Dana handed Alex the hammer, then gazed at Alex's calves. "You've got a nice little muscle right here," she said as she traced it with her finger.

Alex dropped the blanket. "Okay, you can't touch me like that while I'm on a ladder."

"Sorry." Dana picked the corner of the blanket up and handed it to Alex. "Just so we're clear, you're not gonna see Collette again, right?"

Alex was about to hammer the nail and looked down. "I'm not going to see anyone but you, ever. I've waited all my life for this."

Dana melted at Alex's words, and her nerves began to settle.

She reached out to touch Alex's leg again and caught herself just before her fingertips brushed skin. Alex was hammering as though she was preparing for a hurricane and the blankets were their only defense.

"Honey…don't you think two nails are enough?"

"I just didn't want it to fall." Alex climbed down the ladder and moved it. When she was done, the room wasn't pitch-black but dark enough to make Dana happy. "Okay, so…when we want to, we can come in here. Would you like a glass of wine or something else to drink, some grapes?"

They stood staring at each other in the muted light. "Why are we so awkward? I feel kind of like a doofus."

Alex laughed. "I do, too." But she was serious when she said, "This means a lot to me. It's not just sex. So if you feel uncomfortable, I'd be happy just holding you and talking."

Alex stumbled backward and fell onto the bed when Dana sprang on her like a cat. Alex had dreamed of this moment for most of her life, but nothing she mentally conjured compared to Dana actually lying on top of her and delivering kisses that sent jolts of electricity shooting through her body. This is Dana, I'm holding Dana, and she just…oh…bit my neck, Alex thought, temporarily stunned by the overload of pleasurable sensations. Then the urge to explore the woman she'd loved and lusted after almost unbearably took over.

Dana shuddered when cool air met her overheated skin. Alex pulled her shirt off and wasted no time with the bra. Dana was vaguely aware of Alex's hands on her hips moving her up slightly as lips and a tongue moved over the skin of her neck and chest. She sucked in a breath through clenched teeth when a warm mouth closed on one of her nipples. Alex's teeth and tongue teased as her hands slipped down Dana's hips, taking her shorts with them.

"Let me go." Dana moaned.

"What's wrong?"

"Nothing." Dana sat up and started pulling on Alex's shorts. "I just really want to feel you against me."

Alex ripped off her shirt and bra, then kicked out of her shorts and underwear as Dana pulled them down. "Come back to me."

Dana found herself on her back after she climbed back onto the bed. Alex's skin felt like silk as she moved on top of her and settled between her legs. She sucked Alex's tongue deep into her mouth and quickly realized that when she did that, Alex ground into her harder. Dana wrapped her legs around Alex's waist, opening herself up more to her. Alex's moans, her heat, and wetness pressed so firmly against hers drove Dana to heights of arousal she'd never felt before.

Alex wanted to move and taste everything Dana had to offer her, but she was locked in place by Dana's legs wrapped so tightly around her. The friction between them was steadily building a fire inside of her. Dana broke their kisses and grazed her teeth across the skin of her neck, making the intense tension build between Alex's thighs. She gritted her teeth as Dana breathed erratically against her ear, "You're gonna make me come."

Alex's response was a guttural moan that tore through Dana like a bolt of lightning, and the force of it settled right between her legs. Her body tensed so much with the pending orgasm that her back cleared the bed and stole her breath away. Alex continued to grind into her steadily, her body was just as rigid. Dana's eyes flew open, unseeing, her cry breathless as wave after wave rocked her.

She fell back onto the bed weak and held Alex as tight as she could. "Don't stop," she hissed against Alex's ear. "I want to feel you come against me." Dana was stunned by how much she meant that. She gripped Alex's hair with one hand and dug her fingers into the skin of her back with the other. She was amazed that something so erotic could make her want to cry at the same time as she listened to Alex's breathing catch. This is how it feels to love someone so completely, this is the connection, Dana thought, as the orgasm rocked them both.

The urgency between them was gone, and in its place

was the need to languidly map out every sensitive place on their bodies. Alex breathed in the scent of Dana, cataloging in her memory every little muscle twitch, soft sigh, and sharp inhalation as she kissed and tasted the skin of her abdomen. Her lips trailed over the soft curve of a hip bone, noting the thrust of Dana's hips was steadily growing more insistent. She moved lower, slipping her shoulders between Dana's thighs. Alex groaned at the first taste that would always be hers from then on.

She paid close attention to Dana's response to each stroke, memorizing what made her writhe. She coerced and teased until Dana's hand moved into her hair and gripped it tightly. Then Alex focused on the place she knew would give her what she and Dana wanted. Dana gave it up much too easily and quickly. Alex closed her eyes and moaned softly at the tremors against her tongue.

"Come here," Dana breathed out a few minutes later.

Alex crawled up the length of Dana's body and lay halfway on top of her, showering her with little kisses. "I love you," she whispered with a contented sigh.

Dana's fingers grazed the skin of her back. "I love you so very much. I regret that it took me so much time to figure that out. Sydney's right, I am slow." She closed her eyes and sighed when she shifted her leg and felt Alex's wetness against her thigh. "Roll onto your back," she said as she gave Alex a gentle push.

"You—"

Dana put a finger to Alex's lips. "I don't want to hear you say, 'You don't have to do this or that' because that translates to me that you fear I won't enjoy making love to you." She ran her fingertip lightly over Alex's parted lips. "I am going to love every single second because being like this with you feels more natural than any encounter I've ever had. Now lay down."

Alex was beginning to realize that her eyebrows were going to spend a lot of time at her hairline as she got to know this side of Dana. She rolled onto her back, and Dana straddled her thighs. She released a shuddering breath as Dana ran her fingertips lightly over her chest and stomach, avoiding her breasts.

"Do you know what excites me?"

Alex's voice was raspy with desire as she whispered, "Tell me."

"I have a whole list." Dana leaned down and kissed the skin of Alex's neck. "That I make you wet is one." She kissed her way down Alex's chest and flicked her tongue over one of Alex's nipples, then grazed it with her teeth, eliciting a moan. "That." Dana slipped one leg between Alex's and sucked her nipple into her mouth and added a little pressure with her teeth. Alex's hips moved beneath her. She likes that, Dana thought as she moved to the other breast and treated it the same.

"I love that you are going to give all your control over to me," Dana whispered as her fingers trailed down Alex's stomach. She breathed against Alex's skin as her fingers slipped into her wetness. "This excites me."

Alex inhaled sharply and groaned when Dana slipped inside of her. "Dana," she whispered on a sigh.

Dana moved lower as she filled Alex. "This makes me want to come," Dana said before she ran her tongue over Alex's clit. "Think about nothing else but giving me what I want."

Another moment of clarity washed over Dana as she stroked Alex with her tongue. She enjoyed the act immensely, loved the intimacy of it, thrilled at the reactions she got out of Alex as she listened to the sound of her breathing and noticed how her hips moved when the right spot was touched. She was again stunned at how natural making love to Alex felt.

"Stay right there," Alex breathed out.

The simple request sent a jolt of desire through Dana. She wanted to make Alex come, wanted to feel it against her tongue. As Alex tensed, Dana felt exhilaration with the knowledge that she was pleasing Alex that way. Alex's entire body became taut, and her heels dug into the bed as the orgasm shot through her.

"Oh, wow! That was a rush. Let go of my head, I want to do that again," Dana said as she pushed at Alex's hand.

"I need a minute...Dana...that's sensitive."

"Three more, and I'll be happy."

"Three! Are you...oh!"

"You are an extremely sexy lover." Alex kissed Dana's lips before feeding her a grape.

Dana looked away as her face warmed. "You make me feel that way."

"After all the things you said to me, are you going to blush now?" Alex asked with a laugh and nuzzled the side of Dana's face.

Through the windows of the loft, Dana watched the light of the afternoon slowly fade. Its warm glow filled the house, as soft music played in the living room below. "This is the perfect place to watch a sunset. Why didn't we come here instead of Dune Road that night?"

Alex fed her another grape. "You suggested it. I would've sat with you at the town dump with a clothespin on my nose if that would've made you happy."

Dana laughed as she turned and met Alex's eye before allowing her gaze to roam over the thin tank top and skimpy pair of underwear Alex wore. "Your body is amazing."

Alex tugged on the hoodie Dana had swiped from her. "Yours is perfection. When are you going to stop being self-conscious with me?"

"When you gain weight and get some stretch marks."

"I have those." Alex lay on the nest of blankets they made in the otherwise empty loft. She rolled on her side and smacked her ass. "Look at the backs of my thighs and my hips."

Dana grinned as she took a drink of water. "Oh, I'm looking. Stay like that, this could take a while. I wish I had more time."

Alex rolled back over, sat up and stared into Dana's eyes. "We know each other better than anyone else. Right?"

"Right." Dana pressed a grape into Alex's mouth.

"You're in love with me."

Dana smiled. "Very right."

"I'm in love with you, so…am I being too pushy when I say I want you to move in with me?"

"No, I don't consider that pushy," she said as she popped a grape into her mouth. "And I want to. I need a little time, Alex, but not because I'm unsure about us. Dad and I are restoring our relationship, and I'm not sure how he's going to take the news about this. I'm not ashamed to tell him…I just want a little time with him and you before I reveal something that could make life really tense."

Alex nodded as she studied Dana's face. "I understand that."

Dana gave her a sweet kiss. "Thank you, love."

"Now let's get back to our discussion about your shyness," Alex said as she tried to lift the bottom hem on the hoodie.

Dana grabbed her hand and pushed it away. "If you want to get next to what's underneath it, we need to go back to your room." She stuffed a grape between Alex's lips. "When I feel more confident, you can see it, and you can do absolutely whatever you want with it." Dana threw her head back and laughed when the grape popped back out of Alex's mouth.

Chapter 17

"I am so sore." Lisa stood and rubbed her lower back with both hands. "Clint and I helped his sister and her husband move into the house they just built over the weekend. Everything they have is heavy, even the salt and pepper shakers. She's into that...I don't know what you call it, it's not Victorian or Goth, but all of their things are like pewter. They've even got a suit of armor, and the damn arm fell off. We spent half a day looking for it, and somehow, it got stuffed in a toilet brush holder. Clint wouldn't own up to it, but that's something he would do."

Lisa's blathering faded into the background as Dana tried to hold her eyelids up with her fingertips. She understood all about being sore but couldn't wait to get back to Alex that evening. Their good night kiss that occurred at two in the morning lasted an hour. Alex and Dana agreed that she was going to out herself if she kept staying out like that. Sooner or later, her father would put two and two together. Dana didn't want to neglect Sydney, either, so they came up with a brilliant idea. Dana would have dinner with the family, and when everyone turned in, she'd sneak out and go to Alex. As long as she was back in the house before everyone got up, her plan would work just fine.

"...to see Alex. Are you comfortable with that?"

Dana's head snapped up. "What?"

"I asked you if you'd be comfortable in here by yourself

while I went to see Alex. I think I've pulled a muscle in my back."

Everything that Lisa had said about Alex went zipping through Dana's mind as she chewed her bottom lip.

"Did you…did you just growl?" Lisa asked.

Dana put a hand over her mouth. "Excuse me. Breakfast gave me indigestion. You know…she's probably gonna tell you to take a hot bath and maybe take one of those over-the-counter anti-inflammatory pills. You should try that before you pay for a doctor's visit."

"I did that last night, and none of it worked. I can barely sit in that chair now." Lisa let out a groan that sounded like a mewl and grinned. "Besides, she'll have to examine me. I don't mind having her hands all over my back. I may tell her I pulled a groin muscle." Lisa's brow furrowed. "Was that another burp? You want a Tums or something?" Without waiting for an answer, Lisa said, "I really need to go now. If you're not ready to wing it by yourself for a while, I can have Clint come in."

"No, no, I've got this. But if it's that serious, you should really try to get in with Dr. Morris since he's the doctor. Maybe he can do more for you."

Lisa waved her off as she limped to the door. "What I need are muscle relaxers and a good old-fashioned groping from hottie pants. I'll be back soon."

"And I will stuff you in the big freezer downstairs," Dana said lowly when the door closed. She grabbed her cellphone and sent Alex a hasty text. *Lisa is on her way over. DO NOT SEE HER. Make Dr. Morris do it.*

Dana was dragging by the time she got home that evening. As she walked in the back door, Clara was already preparing to set the table. "Let me help you," Dana said as she took a stack of plates from her. "Sydney texted me and said she'd be working the dinner shift, so she'll be home later."

"You must be so proud of her," Clara said. "She takes every shift they offer when she could be just enjoying the summer.

I don't know many kids her age that have that kind of work ethic."

"She's like her mother."

Dana was surprised by the comment Daniel offered as he walked into the kitchen. "Thanks, Dad," she said with a smile.

He sank into his favorite chair at the table with a weary sigh. "The garden looks outstanding. Your grandmother would be so proud. I'm reminded of my childhood every time I look at it." Daniel offered her a smile; they were becoming more frequent. "Thank you."

Dana went with a compulsion and kissed his cheek. "Thank you for giving me that gift."

Clara released a little sigh as she set a serving dish on the table. Dana glanced at her and noticed her watery eyes. "Onions, they really get to me," Clara said as she quickly turned away.

Once everything was on the table, they sat and began passing dishes. "Sydney told me that she had a wonderful time skiing over the weekend," Daniel said.

Dana nodded. "She and Julia kind of made me nervous jumping the wake like they did. Julia wiped out so badly I was afraid that she'd broken her neck. She just laughed it off. Thank God they're still kind of rubbery at that age."

"You fell down the stairs once. I believe you were around ten," Daniel said as he narrowed his eyes in thought. "Aside from a knot on your elbow, you were fine. You didn't cry until your mother told you that we were taking you to the hospital. She was certain that you'd broken something."

"I remember that." Dana smiled. "What we never told y'all was that Mary accidentally pushed me. I'd punched her in the arm and ran. She caught up with me halfway down the stairs…" Dana didn't look at Daniel as she took a bite of her chicken. They'd not spoken of Mary since she'd returned. There was a time she didn't mention her sister's name at all because Daniel's mood went from bad to intolerable.

"Audrey and I suspected that she had something to do with it, even though both of you denied her involvement. She was at the scene of the crime, so to speak. As I recall, she gave you the radio you always asked her to borrow. I assume that was to pay for your silence."

Daniel met Dana's gaze when she dared to look at him. There was no fury in his eyes; his jaw wasn't set in anger. He'd definitely changed. She relaxed and smiled. "It cost her more than just a radio. I got some clothes out of the deal, too."

"Well played," Daniel said with a nod. "I still believe you'd make a fine attorney."

"Maybe one day I'll go back to school. Right now, my focus is on getting Sydney through high school and into college. I can't express how much your helps means to me while I get back on my feet financially." Dana said next what she swore to herself would never pass her lips. "I'm eternally grateful and indebted to you."

Daniel stared at her for a moment and shook his head. "I'm the one who is in your debt."

Clara sniffed and covered her face with her napkin. "Oh, those onions, what they do to me!"

Alex stared at a bunch of tile samples on her kitchen floor. She considered flooring choices the hardest. Walls and cabinets could be repainted, but once the tile was laid, she'd be stuck with it. She was ready to complete her little love nest now that she could look forward to a future with Dana. At least with it being partially unfinished, Dana could offer input that would make it feel more like home to her. Working on it would give her something to do with her evenings while she waited on Dana to come to her.

When she heard a car door slam, Alex ran onto the deck and met Dana halfway on the stairs. The sparkle in Dana's eyes when she gazed at her made Alex feel like she was going to explode with joy. "I missed you," she said, meaning it with every ounce of her being as she clasped Dana's face in her hands and kissed her.

"Oh, sweetie," Dana said with more kisses. "I missed you, too. How'd you get out of seeing Lisa?"

Alex took her by the hand and headed up the stairs. "Well, I didn't."

Dana slammed on the brakes as soon as they got onto the deck. "What?"

"I left my phone on my desk," Alex explained. "I didn't get your text until the end of the day. Did you just growl?"

"Yes." Dana pulled her hand free of Alex's. "Did she have to take off her shirt?"

"She had on a gown."

Dana pursed her lips as she walked past Alex into the house. "I don't like this."

"I wasn't alone with her. Dot was with me the whole time. She's the nurse I work with."

Dana whirled around with a hand on her hip. "And what does she look like?"

"She's like a hundred and ten." Alex put up her hands. "We need to clear the air on this right now. I see all kinds of people in various states of undress every day. It's part of my job. The only person I want to see naked is you. I understand you don't trust Lisa, and I don't blame you. I have never given you a reason not to trust me, and I never will."

Dana's shoulders sagged. "I'm sorry. I get edgy when I'm tired. You know I'm naturally jealous when it comes to you."

"Yeah, I've got an orange bobcat to prove it." Alex smiled. "Are we okay?"

Dana walked over and kissed her. "We are. How was your day?"

"Good, we stayed busy, and that made the time pass quickly. It dragged once I got home because I couldn't wait to see you. How was yours?"

Dana wrapped her arms around Alex's waist and nuzzled her neck. "It was actually pretty good after Lisa left. It was my first time alone at the helm, and according to Clint, I did a great job. He's going to release me from training early." She sighed. "I'm really looking forward to not having to listen to Lisa."

"I'm proud of you." Alex kissed Dana on the nose and led her to the kitchen and pointed to the samples on the floor. "Do any of these appeal to you?"

Dana walked around them for a few minutes. "I see three that I really like."

"Oh! Let's do this! The names are on the back of each sample." Alex grabbed a piece of paper and a pen and handed it to Dana. "I'm gonna walk out of the room, you write down the ones you like, then we'll see if we picked the same."

"Okay, cool, go." Dana turned over the tiles she liked and noted the names, then she flipped them back over and shuffled them around. "Ready."

Alex returned with a big grin. She picked up three of the tiles she liked most and called out their names. "Earth stone, Aegean gray, and sand."

Dana laughed as she held the paper out, and all three of the same names were listed.

Alex grinned. "Wanna do paint samples now?"

"Oh, fuck, you're so good at this! Alex! Yes!" Dana fell face-first onto the bed in an exhausted heap.

Alex kissed a trail up her spine and over her shoulder. "I'm far from finished with you."

Dana sighed happily. "I don't think we should've brought the paint samples in here. There's one stuck to my face."

Alex's breath fanned over Dana's skin as she laughed. "Whatever it is, let's just go with it. That way, we'll always be reminded of how we chose it." She grunted as she reached out to turn on the bedside lamp. "Roll over and show me what you got."

Dana turned onto her back, and the sample was stuck to her cheek. "Keep your eyes on the chip. What is it?"

"Slate blue, and I like it." Alex's gaze trailed lower. "You have eggplant on your chest. I kind of like that one, too."

"I like the blue."

Alex kissed Dana and pulled the samples from her skin. "Blue it is. Let me check you for more."

Dana bit her bottom lip for a second. "Okay." She watched Alex's face as she moved from on top of her, and her gaze swept over her body. A slight smile graced Alex's face as she moved lower and rubbed her face against Dana's stomach, tracing each stretch mark with her fingers.

"I've never loved anything so perfect in all my life." Alex sighed and gazed up at her. "You are absolutely beautiful. Thank you for this gift. I will always cherish it."

Dana fingered the wispy ends of Alex's hair damp with sweat. "I think you've claimed my entire heart, yet you manage to find little pockets in it and fill them, too."

Alex smiled and lowered her lips to Dana's skin. She covered every mark with tender kisses as she trailed lower. Dana closed her eyes and gave in to the sensation.

"I found dusty dawn, it's kind of pretty."

Dana smiled. "Slate blue."

"Blue it is…can we take the blankets off the windows now?"

"Can we talk about it later?" Dana said with a laugh.

Chapter 18

Alex pulled the chart on the exam room door of her next patient, read over it, and groaned. She opened the door without her usual cheery greeting. "What now?"

Thelma sat on her scooter with a scowl. "Took you long enough, Alexandra. I could've died while I waited."

"Dr. Morris was backed up, so they fit us in with you," Jean explained.

"What's wrong?" Alex asked as she looked at the chart.

"I can't breathe, the reaper's at the door. I feel his cold breath on the back of my neck. My appetite is gone, and I've got the chills. Alex, you've been a shit, but I want you to have my fish-shaped wine bottle collection. Under my bed is a shoebox, there's a naked Barbie doll in there, she's a sixties model. I picked her up at a garage sale, but she didn't have any clothes. I still think she'll go for a good price." Thelma waved a hand. "Now get out that pad of yours and write a prescription for something that's gonna make my passing peaceful."

Alex looked up from the chart. "It says here you're febrile—"

"I am not," Thelma spat out indignantly. "I've got all of my mental faculties."

Alex bit her tongue to keep from laughing. "What that means is that you have a fever."

Thelma glared at her. "Then why didn't you say that?"

"Because I figured you probably didn't know what it meant,

and I was going to make a joke about having to amputate your head, but you interrupted with something I found funnier."

"She started with the fever yesterday," Jean said with a bit of an edge. "If you ever came around, you'd know that. Your dad had to find someone else to help with the cabin y'all were working on. I had vegetables go bad because you weren't around to raid the fridge."

"I've been busy working on the kitchen that you've been complaining about."

"You can still come for dinner at the house. Will you come tonight?"

Alex nodded. "So fever and difficulty breathing, you say?" She began checking Thelma's neck for swollen glands. "What else?"

"Burning in the back of my throat. You choking me ain't making it feel no better."

"You sound a little nasally when you whine. Do you have a runny nose?" Alex asked.

"She went through a box of tissues yesterday." Jean narrowed her eyes. "She leaves a trail of them everywhere she goes."

Alex pressed her stethoscope to Thelma's back. "Deep breath, Maw Maw." She moved it to the other side. "Again."

"I'm gonna pass the hell out if you keep making me do that." Thelma shook her head with a rueful expression. "You ought to be ashamed for putting a dying woman through this."

Alex repeated the process on Thelma's chest and sighed. "No one that smokes as much as you do should have lungs sound that clear. Be honest, are you an alien lovechild? Only that could explain your indestructability."

Thelma wagged a finger. "Okay, you don't get the Barbie doll."

Alex bent at the knees and looked Thelma in the eye. "You're not dying, you have a sinus infection. You have snot. The scrip I'm going to write will be for antibiotics and something to dry you out. You can't drink with it."

"The hell you say. People drink hot toddies when they're sick with this shit. Jean, we need to stop at the store for bourbon, honey, and lemons."

Jean ignored Thelma and asked, "Alex, have you been sick?"

"I'm fine, why?"

"Because you look like shit." Jean moved in close and patted the skin beneath Alex's eyes. "You've got dark rings, and you look like you've lost weight."

It was true, she'd lost five pounds over the last month, between working on the kitchen and Dana working on her. Alex turned and busied herself with Thelma's chart. "The construction stirs up dust, and it irritates my sinuses. I'm fine."

"Good," Thelma said with a nod. "Be on time for dinner, we're having chicken soup and hot toddies."

Jean stared at Alex as they cleaned up after dinner. "Something's going on with you that you're not telling me."

"I'm tired, Mom, that's all it is. Would you put on a pot of coffee?" Alex asked as she wiped down the kitchen table.

"I will not." Jean tossed a pot in the sink. "You stand there looking like shit, telling me you're tired, and you want coffee at eight o'clock at night?" She stalked over to Alex and got in her face. "When you're wrestling with something, that line between your brows gets deep. I have to beg you to talk to me, and when you finally relent and get it out, that line goes away. So out with it, girl."

Alex's well of excuses had run dry, and her patience was running a little thin. She felt like a fool to consider complaining about nonstop sex, but that was all she and Dana did. Alex wanted to talk, plan a future. She wanted to go to bed with Dana, wake up with her, and do mundane things like drink coffee and plan a day off. Dana's response whenever Alex brought up the future was "just a little longer." That was followed by a story of how she and Daniel had a nice conversation, but their talks were nothing of substance, usually just Daniel sharing a memory.

"Alexandra, are you standing there asleep?"

"No, I was lost in thought," Alex snapped and immediately regretted it. "Mom, I'm sorry. I'm just very tired."

Jean pulled a chair out from the table. "Would you sit down for a moment, please?"

Alex sank down.

"Tell me right this minute what's going on with you," Jean said firmly as she sat beside her. "Don't get up until you do."

Alex smiled. "I'm pregnant, and it's Dana's."

"You're testing my patience, child."

"It's kind of true, except for the pregnancy part. I am sleeping with Dana. I'd like to call it a relationship. I love her, she loves me, but things are kind of complicated."

Jean shook her head impatiently. "Stop feeding me bullshit, Alexandra."

Alex met her gaze wearily. "That's the truth."

Jean looked truly stunned. "How long has this been going on?"

"A few weeks.. Dana and I have loved each other for a long time, but she has recently come to terms with it. Things have been going well with her and Daniel, and she doesn't want to rock the boat, so we haven't told anyone about our relationship."

"Then why don't you look happy?"

"I get an average of four hours of sleep a night. I'm exhausted. She's totally unaffected. She can go and go, and God help me, go. I've never met anyone with that kind of stamina. She's like a teenager," Alex said with a pained expression. "When I'm tired, I can't reason very well, and I'm impatient. It's only been a month. No one forced me to come out. I did it when I was ready, so I can't rush her."

"You can tell her to stay outta your damn pants."

Alex closed her eyes and clutched her forehead. "Oh, my God."

"Momma! Are you eavesdropping again?" Jean barked.

Thelma rolled through the door between the den and the kitchen with a grin. "I fell asleep, I'll have you know, and when I woke up, I heard her say she was pregnant. Of course, I listened, who wouldn't?" She waved a finger at Alex. "If you're gonna give out your ass like a hooker on dollar day, don't whine about being tired. She's got herself a new toy, and if you keep letting her play with it, she's gonna get bored with it real quick. You gotta ration that thing, girl."

Jean sighed. "This is one of those rare instances that I'm gonna admit Momma has a point."

Thelma wheeled over next to Alex. "So you finally got the girl. I'm impressed. I didn't think you had a snowball's chance in hell."

Chagrined that Thelma was now part of the conversation, Alex replied, "Neither did I."

Jean patted the table with her hand. "I need you to go back to the part where you said Dana just came to terms with loving you. What exactly does that mean?"

Alex knew she was stepping on a landmine by answering, but the cat was out of the bag. "This is the condensed version. She realized that there was no one she'd ever connected with except for me. She recognized lesbian tendencies in herself, but she shelved them because she was focused on raising Sydney. When we reunited, it was like an epiphany. Trust me when I say she is a lesbian."

"Ah, she's a girl who likes her muffin," Thelma said with a nod and a wink. "Or better yet, yours."

Alex sounded like she'd regressed back to a ten-year-old. "Mom, make her stop."

"Momma!"

"Hey! I could be one of those old stodgy disapproving biddies. But I'm cool. I'm down with it...not down that way, but you feel me, right...probably shouldn't have used that term with a lesbian, either." Thelma looked proud of herself when she said, "I've been watching *MTV Cribs*, I'm hip on the jargon. I've got the youthful tongue...shiat! That wasn't a good one to use, either."

Jean stared at her mother for a moment, then turned to Alex. "Honey, do you know what you're doing?"

"Obviously, she does if she's only getting four hours of sleep a night."

"Momma!"

Thelma slapped the handlebar of her scooter and hit the throttle. It lurched forward, and one of the wheels rolled over Alex's foot. "Again?" Alex bellowed.

Alex noticed that Dana's jaunt up her stairs each night had gradually gone from a run to a walk, and that particular evening, she got halfway up and took a break.

"Baby, would you mind if tonight we just snuggled and slept for a change?"

Alex gripped the railing and lifted her face to the sky. "Oh, thank God, I'm pretty much punch-drunk from exhaustion."

"Well, you could've told me," Dana said with a weary laugh as she continued up the stairs.

Alex took Dana's hand and kissed it when she reached the top. "How long do you think we can keep this up?"

"I've thought about that, too," Dana admitted with reluctance as they walked inside and sat on the couch. "I know I need to talk to Dad, really talk about a lot of things. It's been pleasant, but there seems to be a wall still between us. It's as though we're trying so hard to be nice that we can't be ourselves. I'm just afraid that when I tell him I'm going to find the man I knew lurking behind that sweet façade." Dana rubbed the back of her neck and looked down. "I need to tell you something else."

Alex put her finger beneath Dana's chin until she met her eye. "You can tell me anything."

"I'm also struggling with the fact that I have a lot of debt, and I'm not alone. There's Sydney to consider. Nearly all of my paychecks go toward my car note and credit cards. I can't contribute anything to our household."

"I already figured that. You wouldn't be living with your father otherwise. I'll do the same thing he's doing. I'll take care of our expenses, you take care of the debt. When you're paid up, we'll put that money in savings and use it for whatever Sydney needs or travel. And as far as Sydney goes, she has her choice between the two bedrooms down here or the loft. This is her home, too."

"I—"

Alex put a finger to Dana's lips. "When you say things like, 'I don't want to take advantage of you' or 'I don't feel right about this,' that translates to me that you fear that I'll resent taking care of you. I never will. What I need to know is if you have faith in us as a couple and you want to live with me."

"I trust you, and I have confidence in us, and with all my heart, I want to live with you for the rest of my life." Dana smiled into Alex's kiss. "The wallpaper in the guest bathroom has to go."

Alex regarded her seriously. "The pineapples haven't grown on you?"

"Not even a little."

Dana laughed when Alex cracked up. "You are so damn adorable. You make me want you all the time."

"We are sleeping tonight. Maw Maw says I need to ration my 'thing,' and I think she may've called me a hooker, but I was too tired to truly comprehend."

Dana sat straight up. "You told Thelma?"

Alex grimaced. "She overheard me talking to Mom."

"You told Jean?" Dana asked, looking horrified.

"Honey, they're not going to tell anyone."

"But…but you told them we were having so much sex that they suggested you ration it?"

Alex's face went blank. "I…um…yeah because mom demanded to know why I looked so tired, and I may've mentioned you are insatiable."

Dana's mouth fell open. "You told your momma that I'm some sort of horny beast?"

Alex wagged a finger. "I did not use those words. I just said you could go on forever."

Dana's gasp sounded like a squeak.

"Baby, people in relationships have sex. Without me saying so, she knows. Mom's not shy about talking about sex. When I was with Vanessa, she—"

"Oh, no!" Dana waved her hands. "You can't use sex and Vanessa's name in the same sentence with me. As far as I'm concerned, you were a virgin before I got a hold of you, and you can think the same of me."

Alex bit her lip as she laughed.

"I can't believe you told your momma I was a hypersexual. I have to face her, you know. I'm sure you didn't bother to add that there are times you ply me with coffee to keep me going. Your punishment is to carry me into the bedroom because I'm too tired to walk." Dana poked Alex in the ass when she flopped over laughing.

"Baby, pick me up."

"Let's just sleep here."

Chapter 19

The last few days of June were hot. Dana watered the garden in the cool of a Saturday morning, pleased that the clematis had really taken off and was climbing the gate posts. The hydrangeas were in bloom, butterflies visited the bottlebrushes in the corners, and the vegetable plants were producing.

"It's so lush and lovely. Your grandmother would be very proud."

Dana turned and smiled at her father. "Does it look like hers?"

"Very much so." Daniel leaned heavily on his cane as he gazed at it. "You've brought one of my fondest memories back to life."

"I've enjoyed every second. This has meant a lot to me, too."

Daniel met her eye. "Are you happy here?"

That was a question she wasn't sure how to answer. "Yes… I am. You've made Sydney and I both feel very welcome."

"You're still a young woman. I imagine living with your father does put a crimp in your lifestyle. I want you to know that you are welcome to stay here as long as you want, it is your home."

This was the perfect segue. Dana felt her mouth go dry. "Thank you. I do want to stay in Barbier Point. Alex and I have…" Dana clammed up when she saw Clara headed toward them with a phone in her hand.

Always Alex

"This is Nate," she said softly as she handed the phone to Daniel. "One of his boys is having a problem, he needs your professional advice."

Dana watched as her father walked off, her insides quivering. She'd come so close and wasn't sure she actually had the nerve to go through with it. She blew out a breath as Sydney walked out the back door and held it for her grandfather as he went inside.

"What're your plans today?" Dana asked as Sydney walked up.

"Nothing. I'm off, and Julia's on a camping trip."

"Do you want to come with me to Alex's? We're going to be harvesting some pineapples in her bathroom."

"Yeah, sure. You okay?"

"I almost just told your grandpa about my relationship with Alex, but we were interrupted. I'm disappointed and relieved all at the same time."

Sydney tossed her head and flipped her brown bangs out of her eyes. "I think he's gonna be cool with it."

Dana sighed. "He may surprise me." Dana repositioned the sprinkler. "Alex and I have been talking. She wants us to move in with her, and I want to. How do you feel about it?"

Sydney shrugged. "I like Alex, I think it'd be cool. It's gonna make me kinda sad to leave Grandpa."

"We wouldn't be leaving him. We're less than ten minutes away at Alex's place. I plan to visit him a lot unless…"

"I know," Sydney said with a nod. "If he rejects you, he'll be rejecting me. I think about those things."

"I'm sorry you have to," Dana admitted sadly.

Sydney shrugged. "One day, it won't matter. People will just see us as people."

Alex and Sydney giggled as they cut the pineapples out of the wallpaper while Dana scraped at the pieces that didn't come off easily. "I think whoever put this crap up used superglue," Dana fussed.

"Need me to take over, baby?" Alex held a finger to her lips when Sydney snorted.

"No, it's pissing me off. I can't let it defeat me."

Sydney pulled Dana's wallet out of her purse and slipped the pineapples in every slot. The wallet was brimming with them. Then she opened every zippered compartment in Dana's purse and slipped them in as fast as Alex could cut them out of the paper.

"Keep cutting," Sydney whispered. "I'm gonna put a bunch in her car, so you keep her distracted."

"What're y'all doing?" Dana called out.

"I'm...uh...looking for another scraper, so I can help. Sydney's helping me."

Alex grinned when Sydney snickered. She took the scissors from Alex and a big piece of the wallpaper and went outside. Alex joined Dana in the bathroom.

"Oh, you're a killer, you're a beast. Get that pesky pineapple, baby!"

"You're coming down," Dana ground out as she went at it with gusto. "Oh, hey, I talked to Sydney about us moving in with you. She's onboard. For some strange reason, she likes you."

"I'm super fond of her, too. She may look like her father, but that personality of hers is all Dana. This is good news. Can I go ahead and tell her she can pick out a room?"

Dana looked over her shoulder with a smile. "Sure, baby."

"Hello?"

"We're in the bathroom, Mom," Alex called out.

"Oh, my God! There's a kitchen in here, and it's pretty. It looks like civilized human beings actually live here. My daughter must've moved out."

Alex laughed as she grabbed Dana by the hand, and they joined Jean as she gave herself a tour.

"Are you happy now?" Alex asked, very pleased with the way it turned out. The walls were slate blue, and the cabinets and tile countertops were white, as were the appliances. Dana and Alex finally agreed on the earth stone for the floor, which was basically a sand color with gray touches.

"And you two did this all by yourselves?" Jean asked as she admired it all.

"No, Alex did all of it. I helped her paint a little bit and move the appliances in."

Jean turned and looked at Dana with a smug smile. "When did you two possibly have the time?"

Dana's face flushed. "Umm…"

Jean laughed and pulled her in for a hug.

"I am not the animal your daughter claims I am," Dana said when Jean released her.

"Yes, she is."

Dana laughed and pointed a finger at Alex. "You hush."

"I came over here to see the kitchen and to tell you two that your presence is required at the house on the Fourth of July. We will be having a daylong get-together and fireworks that night. Dana, I want to invite your father and Clara, are you okay with that?"

"Sure." Dana glanced at Alex. "I haven't told him about what's going on between me and Alex yet, though."

"It's just gonna be us and the Satterwhites. No one is going to say anything. Can you two keep your hands off each other for a day?"

"I can, but I don't know about the horny beast hypersexual." Alex laughed when Dana glared at her.

Dana turned and smiled at Jean. "We'll be fine because she's gonna be begging for the horny beast by then."

Jean winked at Alex. "I think you just got yourself cut off." She kissed Dana on the cheek, then Alex. "I'm going home to make my menu for the party, and I'll give your dad a call and invite him."

Sydney walked in just as Jean headed for the door. "Good to see you again, Sydney. Plan to be at my house for a party on the Fourth. I know the diner's closed then."

"Okay, I'll be there," Sydney said as she grinned at Alex.

Dana watched them for a second as they tried to keep from laughing. "This can't be good."

Sydney threw an arm over Alex's shoulders. "We're just happy to see each other."

"Oh, hey, you need to pick out a bedroom, and if you want it to be something besides white, you need to pick a color," Alex said to Sydney.

"And if you go with a color, *you'll* need to paint it," Dana added.

"What if I painted something on the white?" Sydney asked excitedly. "Like the silhouette of a movie camera and film?"

"I think that'd be cool," Alex said, sounding just as excited. "You could do the film as a border midway up the wall. We could just tape it off to make sure it's even and make the frames."

"I like that idea. Can I have the room behind the kitchen? I really don't wanna be next to y'all, no offense." Sydney glanced at Dana. "I don't wanna hear anything."

"Room behind the kitchen it is, let's go measure," Alex said as they walked off.

Dana watched her girls go with a smile. She'd never felt more alive or happier. There was one little fly in the ointment, and it walked with a cane.

Alex, Dana, and Sydney spent the entire day together and most of the evening. The three of them had cooked dinner in the newly renovated kitchen, then watched a movie. Afterward, Dana got ready to go. Sensing that they wanted a moment alone, Sydney went into what was to be her new room.

Alex pulled Dana into her arms and said, "You're not coming back tonight, are you?"

"No. I know you're ready for me to tell him. I had a chance this morning, and I started to when we were interrupted by a call he had to take. I know I'm being selfish. It's just been so long since he and I have been civil. I can't deny the chance of messing that up breaks my heart, but I want to be here with you so badly."

Alex kissed Dana's forehead. "Baby, I'm not pushing. I understand how you feel. You do it when you're ready. I will wait for you as long as it takes."

"You mean that, don't you?" Dana stroked Alex's cheek.

"With all my heart."

Chapter 20

Days went by, and Dana's stress level rose with every one that passed. The conversation she knew she needed to have with her father loomed over her head like a storm cloud and seemed to grow bigger and heavier with each minute that ticked by. She found herself staring at him with such a mixture of emotions. She didn't want to hurt him; she didn't want him to hurt her or Sydney. She'd lost so much time with Alex over the years and her father, too. Alex was patient and supportive, but even still, Dana felt like she had to choose between them, but the choice had already been made.

Dana gazed at him the morning of the Fourth as they finished breakfast. "What time are you coming to the Soileaus today?"

"I told Jean that Clara and I would be there for dinner. I'd like to see the fireworks, but I don't have it in me to stay all day and into the night. What are your plans?"

"Sydney and I are gonna go over in a little while. We're gonna hang out by the pool and get some sun."

Daniel set his fork to the side and took a sip of his coffee. "I'm glad you have such a wonderful friend in Alex. I've always been fond of her."

Clara had already gotten up and was cleaning some of the dishes. Dana knew that her father would not appreciate having a conversation like the one they needed to have in front of her. But Dana was tempted to test the waters. "Does her being a lesbian offend you?"

Daniel gazed at her for a moment. "Not at all. As I said, I've always been fond of her. She's a good woman."

Dana smiled as a tiny wave of relief washed over her. "She's very dear to me, too."

Sydney strolled into the kitchen with a backpack slung over her shoulder. "I'm ready to sun my buns."

Dana stood and gathered her dishes. "Are you done, Dad?"

"I am, thank you."

Dana stared at him for a moment and kissed his cheek. "I love you, Daddy."

He stared at her in surprise as she stood up straight. "I love you, too, I always have," he said with sincerity in his watery blue eyes.

Dana gulped at the ball of emotion that formed in her throat and gathered his dishes. When she took them to the sink, Clara was wiping her eyes. "Onions," she rasped. "Go on, honey, I've got these dishes," she said when Dana tried to put them in the washer.

"I'll see y'all a little later then," Dana said as she picked up her bag.

Daniel was still staring at her. "I look forward to it," he said with a smile.

"That was a big moment," Sydney said as Dana pulled to the end of the driveway, and a little sob escaped her.

"I was fourteen the last time I heard him say that." Dana turned and looked at Sydney. "I love you. Do you ever have any doubts?"

Sydney shook her head. "Never once."

Dana smiled and swallowed hard. She wiped her eyes with the back of her hand, then pulled her sunglasses down from where they were hooked to her visor. Two pineapples were stuck to the lenses. Over the past week, she'd found the infernal things in just about everything she owned. The topper was when Alex met her at the door one night topless with them taped over her nipples.

"If I find another one of these things, you and Alex will each eat half," Dana said as she tossed them at Sydney.

"Okay, maybe I'm doubting a little bit right now."

Skies overhead were blue, the sun was bright, Alex and Dana sat side by side on lounges as they watched the spectacle in the pool. Thelma floated fully clothed on her back in the water while Sydney pushed her around by her feet. A black wiglet drifted on the waves they caused.

"She's like a barge," Alex whispered.

Dana shook her head. "I've never seen a human float like that, and I don't remember her having a mole on her cheek."

"That's not a mole, I think it's a raisin." Alex took Dana's hand. "Are you ready to tell me why you looked like you were crying when you got here?"

"I think I can manage without bursting into tears again," Dana said with a sigh. "Dad told me he loved me today, and he got a little misty-eyed." She turned to Alex. "Do you know how long it's been since he said that?"

Alex nodded. Her lip quivered as she looked away.

"Oh, no, you can't do that. You're gonna stir me up again. I don't wanna be bug-eyed all day."

"I just know how much that means to you," Alex said with a little gasp.

"Before that," Dana said tearfully, "I asked him if he had a problem with you being gay, just testing the waters, and he said not at all." She sniffed and squeaked out, "He said not at all, and he was always fond of you and you are a good woman."

Alex wrapped her arms around Dana. "I'm so happy for you."

"Why are you two yowling like a couple of stray cats at a fish market?" Thelma asked. "Aw, shiat! Sydney, get my wiglet out of the intake basket, would ya?"

Daniel and Clara were treated like royalty when they arrived later that afternoon. Jean fawned over them both, making sure they had plenty to drink and the most comfortable of her patio chairs to sit in. She even set up a fan to blow directly on Daniel to keep him cool.

"Is it my imagination or is your mom doting on my dad more than usual?" Dana asked as she stood beside Alex at the grill.

"Yeah, she's pouring it on. I'd like to think she's just so happy to have him back over here. If you think about it, our families haven't gotten together like this since Mary died. I know Mom has invited him over a lot of times, but he never accepted." Alex smiled sadly. "I'm sure being here reminds him of the past, maybe he couldn't handle that until now."

Dana began chewing on her bottom lip as she nodded. Alex watched her for a moment, wanting to pull her close and whisper that everything was going to be fine, but she couldn't do either. She had no clue how Daniel would react to their relationship. Alex wanted to believe he'd be accepting and everyone would live happily ever after. There was just a nagging fear that Daniel might snatch away the wish that she'd been granted.

"I think Clara is kind of smitten with him," Dana said with a slight smile. "I think it would be kind of sweet if they got together."

"They kind of are a couple in a way." Alex turned some of the meat on the grill and gazed at Daniel and Clara sitting side by side. "They take care of each other, go places together. I know for Christmas he gave her the pair of earrings she always wears. She showed them off to everyone in the office when they came in for an appointment."

"Aw," Dana said with a winsome smile. "Maybe we aren't the only two secretly in love."

Alex's brow furrowed when she noticed that Clara had gotten up and gone inside with Jean. Thelma was making her way over to Daniel. "You should probably go see about your dad." Alex looked a little worried when she turned to Dana. "There's no telling what she'll say to him."

"Good point." Dana headed toward her father, but Thelma had already wheeled in beside him, and she was talking up a storm.

"...so after I had the colitis, everything I eat gives me terrible gas. My stomach just bloats up like a basketball, and I have no control. It's hard to hide a fart when your ass is stuck to a vinyl seat. I had myself a horn, and I'd toot it whenever I broke wind to hide the sound. Some days, the gas was so bad, I sounded like I was in a traffic jam. Someone stole it off my scooter, and no one has confessed to it, but I have three prime suspects—Bert, Ernie, and Kermit over there behind the grill."

Daniel's lips were parted, his eyes as wide as saucers.

Dana saved him from trying to respond and said, "Mrs. Thelma, are you telling Dad about the owls?"

"No, I was just getting around to telling him about the fact that I'm dying. My ol' system is steadily shutting down. My stools are white now. A couple of weeks ago, I coughed up—"

"Oh!" Daniel said and struggled to get up. "I just remembered that I need to take my blood pressure medicine. Clara has it, just let me go and find her."

Dana clamped her lips together tightly to keep from laughing. "She's in the kitchen with Jean."

"Do you know what I just realized?"

Alex glanced at Thelma. "I'm afraid to ask."

"I'm at the damn kids' table."

It was true and intentional. Jean had very carefully arranged the tables on the patio and told Alex and Dana they were in charge of corralling Thelma during dinner. So they, along with Sydney and Julia, sat together with Thelma, while Alex's parents, Daniel, and Clara, along with Kyle and Patty Satterwhite, sat at another one on the other side of the patio.

"Dana and I aren't kids." Alex picked up a rib and shot Dana a little smile.

"You're fleas in my old eyes," Thelma huffed. "I was around long before you got here. I remember coming for a visit and you'd just been born, Dana. Alex was two. Your momma brought you over here wrapped in a pink blanket, and she was so proud. She put you in my arms, and I remember looking at your little face thinking you looked like a pale prune. And Alex's head was huge. She toddled around like a drunk because she could barely hold that thing up. Y'all were some ugly-ass children."

"And this would be why you're at the kids' table," Alex said as Sydney and Julia laughed hysterically.

Dana watched Daniel as he talked with the others while they ate. He was more animated than she'd seen him since she'd been home. He laughed at something Wade said, and Dana smiled as her mind drifted back to another time. She could see much younger versions of Wade, Jean, Daniel, and her mother, Audrey, sitting in lawn chairs with the late summer sun shining on their faces as they laughed and talked. Dana could picture Mary, Andrew, and Malcolm sticking close together and running her and Alex off because they were younger and annoying. It was a happy memory tinged with sadness because the group now was incomplete.

Dana blinked when she realized her father was looking directly at her. She returned his smile. An odd feeling settled inside of her, a knowing that everything was going to be okay. Beneath the table, Alex's hand found hers, and Dana smiled again, reminded that she could look forward to making more precious memories.

As night fell, the fireworks began. Wade, Kyle, and the girls set them off, while Thelma griped that no one would let her have a Roman candle. Alex got up and went into the house, and Dana, who wanted to steal a kiss, followed.

Dana hid in the foyer and waited for Alex to come out of the guest bathroom. When the door opened, Dana sprang out and screamed, then laughed at the scream and dance that Alex did. Alex put a hand on her chest and laughed. "I hope you know payback is going to be a big-time bitch."

Dana sagged against Alex as she laughed. "It'll be so worth it. You should've seen what you did. You threw your hands up and jogged in place for a second. I'm sorry, baby," Dana said as she kissed her lips. "I'll make it up to you later, I promise." Alex's face turned to stone. "Are you mad now?"

But Alex wasn't staring at her, and Dana turned to find Daniel standing in the foyer with them. The cold stare that Dana had hoped she'd never see again was in Daniel's eyes as he regarded them. Dana tried to speak, but words—all thought—had failed her.

"Mr. Castilaw," Alex began as she took a step toward him.

Dana winced at the coldness in Daniel's tone when he said, "Now is not the time."

Mute, Dana watched as he turned and walked through the kitchen. When the back door closed behind him, Alex turned slowly and gazed at Dana with devastation in her eyes. They no longer had to wonder if Daniel would disapprove, he'd made that obvious.

Alex thought it sad that their very first morning waking up in bed together when the sun was out wasn't going to be something they'd feel like celebrating. She gazed at the tension lines on Dana's face as she slept, wondering why joy sometimes came with such a huge cost. She ached for Dana and wanted to hold her but feared that she'd awaken her after a mostly sleepless night. Carefully, she slipped out of bed and crept from the room.

Sydney, who was sleeping on the couch, sat up when Alex ran the water for the coffeemaker. Alex held a finger to her lips, and Sydney nodded, understanding that Dana was still asleep. She tossed a blanket aside and joined Alex in the kitchen.

"How is she?" Sydney asked softly as she ran a hand through her bedhead.

"She didn't sleep much, and she didn't really have any more to say after we went to bed."

"I'm gonna go with her to talk to Grandpa. I don't want her to have to deal with him alone. You should come, too. Mom needs support."

Alex nodded. "I am."

"Neither of you are coming." Alex and Sydney turned and found Dana dressed, her hair in a ponytail. Her eyes were dull, emotionless as she regarded them. "I appreciate that you both are so supportive, but this conversation needs to happen between me and Dad alone. With y'all there, he'll feel ganged up on, and it'll only make him more defensive. If he were to say anything hurtful to either of you, he and I will get into a screaming match, and I won't be able to say everything I need to. So, please, respect my wishes."

"We'll ride over with you then and wait in the car," Alex said.

"No, but thank you. I'll be back in a little while." Dana turned and walked out.

Alex chased after Dana and caught up with her on the stairs. "Can I at least hug you?"

"I have to go while I still have my nerve. If you hug me, I'm going to want to stay in your arms. Kiss me instead."

Alex leaned in and kissed Dana quickly but softly. "I love you."

A little life returned to Dana's eyes. "I love you, too."

Alex stood on the stairs and watched her go, feeling helpless.

Clara was on Dana the second she walked in the back door. "What on earth is going on?" she whispered. She put a hand on Dana's arm. "Did he fall while he was in the house? I know he gets terribly embarrassed when that happens, and I figured that's why he wanted to leave so abruptly last night. He won't tell me a thing."

"He didn't fall, and I really can't explain everything at the moment. Where is he?"

"In his study," Clara said, looking a bit hurt.

The hallway leading to Daniel's study felt like it was a mile long. Her knock and her voice seemed to echo loudly. "Dad, it's Dana."

"Come in."

The mantra that Dana had spoken repeatedly on her drive over began to go through her mind. *Look him in the eye. Show no fear. Don't fidget. Say what you need to say, and don't let him get you off point. Don't cry.*

Dana kept her chin up, her gaze upon his as she sat in the chair across from where he sat on the sofa. "I need to apologize to you. I'm sorry I haven't told you sooner about my relationship with Alex."

Daniel's face looked drawn and tired, his lips twitched slightly before he asked, "Is that how you define it?"

"Actually, I'd go a step further and say that we are in a committed relationship."

One of Daniel's eyebrows arched slightly. "And Sydney, is she aware of this relationship?"

"She is."

Daniel's voice was even when he asked, "And are you concerned about what effect this may have on her?"

"Sydney is also a lesbian."

Daniel's nostrils flared as he exhaled and looked away. "I've made a fine mess of not one, but two generations. I'm angry with myself, not you. I failed you."

"You dropped the ball for a little while, but our history has nothing to do with my sexuality. You've known Jean and Wade for decades. They're wonderful parents, and they have two gay children. There's no sense in trying to figure out how or why. What matters is that Sydney and I are what we are and how you choose to deal with it. I love you. I've enjoyed my time with you, but I will do what I have to do to protect my daughter and myself. If you can't see anything else but our sexuality and that offends you, then we don't have anything else to discuss."

Daniel slowly turned and met Dana's eye. "Well said. May I say my piece now?"

Dana nodded as she steeled herself.

"As a parent, I'm sure you can understand the vulnerability that comes with being one. I've lost my own parents, siblings, my wife, but that pain could not compare to what I felt when I lost a child. It took me a while to figure out that I was not the man I thought I was. I considered myself a leader, the head of this household, and when I needed to be those things the most, I failed. Then I lost both of my children. In my weakness, I believed that it was best to let you go and drift into that place of numbness where I didn't feel anything. I told myself that you were better off without having to deal with such a poor excuse for a father. Your return has been a continual reminder of what a terrible fool I've been," he said, his voice hoarse. "So many wasted years."

Daniel shook his head, leaned forward, and clasped his hands between his knees. "You shocked me last night. I had to have time to absorb it all, and I wasn't even close when you informed me about Sydney a few minutes ago. I'm going to need some time to reconcile this. I did drop the ball, as you put it, and I know I can't just pick it up and run as though nothing ever happened. I have tremendous regret and sorrow over the mess I made of our lives. I am so terribly sorry for what I did to you, what I took away from you. I love you and Sydney with all my heart and soul, and I have no intention of turning my back on the two of you. I just need to trust that you won't give up on me."

Dana pursed her lips and nodded. "Well said." A smile spread across her face as she put out her hand. "I agree to be patient and open as we work through our differences."

"You have my word that I will do the same," Daniel said as he shook her hand. He laughed as he stood and pulled her to him. "We'll discuss law school at another time."

Dana sighed as she hugged him tight. "I need to tell you that Sydney and I are going to move in with Alex. I'm so grateful for what you've done for us, but I hope you can understand that I want to share my life with her."

"I do understand that, accepting it will take a little while. Acceptance will come a lot quicker if you tell me that you'll come for dinner often and tend the garden."

Dana smiled. "I will gladly agree to that."

"Do you have any Xanax?"

Alex stopped pacing and gazed at Sydney with brows raised. "No, why?"

"I was gonna suggest you take one…or six. You've been walking back and forth across the floor so much, I think you're scuffing the finish off."

Alex put both hands in her hair. "I feel like I've sent her off to face a giant alone."

"Mom's tough."

Alex smiled. "I know she is."

"Are you afraid that if Grandpa doesn't approve, Mom will break up with you?"

Alex's "no" was weak. "Have you ever wanted something so bad, and once you get it, you're just afraid that it's going to be snatched away? Like some wishes are so wonderful they can't possibly come true?"

Sydney folded her legs up with her on the sofa and nodded. "You wait for the string attached to be pulled."

"I've loved her for so long, just about all my life." Alex walked over to the window and stared out. "I dumped a fortune in that well, wishing that she would be mine, but I never truly thought it would happen because that wish was just too wonderful to come true. Now…" Alex turned and abruptly walked out of the room.

"Maybe she does have Xanax," Sydney said when she was alone. "She better take more than one, or a vein is gonna pop out of her forehead."

Alex returned a minute or two later with a giant pickle jar

filled halfway with change tucked beneath her arm. "I'll share if you want to make some wishes."

Sydney got up with a grin and followed Alex down to the well. "Aren't you supposed to throw one coin in at a time?" she asked when Alex grabbed a fistful.

"Bring her back to me, you greedy bastard!" Alex yelled and tossed the money in." She grabbed another handful. "I want my happily ever after, and I can't be happy if she isn't happy." Alex stuck her face in the well. "You hear me?"

"Okay, you're kinda cracking up." Sydney tugged the jar from Alex's grasp. "Mom's coming back. No matter what Grandpa says, she's still gonna love you." She pulled out a nickel and tossed it in. "I just wished that Leighton and I are this adorkable when we're old."

Alex's brows shot skyward. "Old? We're not—"

They both turned when Dana's car came roaring up the driveway. It had barely stopped when Dana jumped out and threw her hands in the air. "Honey, I'm home with Clara's chicken salad!"

Alex grinned at Sydney haughtily. "See, I told you not to worry." She raced over to Dana and threw her arms around her. "This is the beginning of our happy ever after."

Epilogue

"Momma bird to crow, is the package in place?" Dana said when Alex answered her phone.

"I told you, it's hawk, and we're set. Is baby bird in the nest?"

Most all of the graduates were seated except for a few stragglers. She hoped when the ceremony began that Sydney would stay facing forward. The "package" would slip in behind Alex and Daniel once the proceedings started.

"Baby bird is in the nest, the principal is coming up to the podium, make your move."

Dana watched as Alex and her father walked down the aisle side by side wearing matching smiles. Alex looked sexy in a navy blue pantsuit, and Daniel, of course, was resplendent in his tan suit. He looked proud to have Alex's hand on his arm.

Daniel's adjustment didn't take long. He finally conceded that as far as mates went, Dana couldn't do any better than Alex. Daniel attended many more cookouts at the Soileaus, and the families reminisced about old gatherings as they made new memories together.

The Soileaus and the Castilaws took up an entire row of chairs in the high school gym when Alex, Leighton, and Daniel sat down. Dana could hear Thelma, who was on the other end say, "Where's the rest of that child? She's as skinny as a garden rake. Sydney better fatten her up."

Dana hugged Leighton and whispered, "I can't believe you skipped your own ceremony to be here."

"It didn't mean anything to me. My whole world is sitting up there," Leighton said with a smile.

Dana gazed at the petite blond with big green eyes and the same short hairstyle that Sydney wore. "She's going to be beside herself when she sees you."

The ceremony seemed like it took forever to Dana. She was eager to see Sydney walk across the stage and realize that Leighton was there. When Sydney's name was finally called, everyone on their row cheered. Sydney accepted her diploma and headed down the steps as she waved, then she froze for a second. The smile she wore grew brighter, and instead of returning to sit with her class, she strode right past their rows and squeezed in between Alex and Leighton. Dana felt her eyes well with tears as Sydney hugged Leighton and shed a few of her own.

Daniel and Clara had pulled out all the stops for the party. A huge banner hung from the balcony over the patio that read: *Congratulations to our graduates, Sydney and Leighton.* They even included Leighton's name on the cake. Clara had the event catered, and there was music and dancing on the patio.

"Are you okay?" Alex asked as she stayed close at Dana's side and handed her another tissue.

"I'm sure I'll stop crying in a few weeks," Dana said with a sniff. "I thought I had composed myself until I saw you get weepy."

Alex jutted her chin. "I did not. I was having an allergic reaction to Maw Maw's perfume, it smells like sandalwood and ham." Her gaze swept over the sleeveless royal blue sheath dress that Dana wore. "Have I told you that you look absolutely stunning today?"

Dana smiled. "At least a dozen times, but I never get tired of hearing it from you."

"You could wear a burlap sack, and I'd think you were gorgeous."

"She is lovely, isn't she?"

Alex and Dana turned to find Daniel standing beside them. "Thank you, Dad," Dana said, warmed by the compliment and his smile. "And thank you for throwing such a wonderful party and for flying Leighton in."

"She's a delightful girl, and it thrills me to see Sydney so happy." Daniel took a handkerchief from his pocket and blotted a tear on Dana's cheek. "And you, too."

Dana smiled and hugged him. "I love you, Dad."

"I love you, too, dear one."

Alex sniffed. "Damn Maw Maw's perfume."

About the Author

Robin Alexander is the author of the Goldie Award-winning *Gloria's Secret* and many other novels for Intaglio Publications—*Gloria's Inn, Gift of Time, The Taking of Eden, Love's Someday, Pitifully Ugly, Undeniable, A Devil in Disguise, Half to Death, Gloria's Legacy, A Kiss Doesn't Lie, The Secret of St. Claire, Magnetic, The Lure of White Oak Lake, The Summer of Our Discontent, Just Jorie, Scaredy Cat,* and *The Magic of White Oak Lake.*

She was also a 2013 winner of the Alice B Readers Appreciation Award, which she considers a true feather in her cap.

Robin spends her days working with the staff of Intaglio and her nights with her own writings. She still manages to find time to spend with her partner, Becky, and their three dogs and four cats.

You can reach her at robinalex65@yahoo.com. You can visit her website at www.robinalexanderbooks.com and find her on Facebook.

For more information on Intaglio
Publications, titles
visit us at
www.intagliopub.com

Printed in Great Britain
by Amazon